Seraphita

Honoré de Balzac

Seraphita

Copyright © 2024 Indo-European Publishing

All rights reserved

The present edition is a reproduction of previous publication of this classic work. Minor typographical errors may have been corrected without note; however, for an authentic reading experience the spelling, punctuation, and capitalization have been retained from the original text.

ISBN: 979-8-88942-400-0

DEDICATION

To Madame Eveline de Hanska, nee Comtesse Rzewuska

Madame,—Here is the work which you asked of me. I am happy, in thus dedicating it, to offer you a proof of the respectful affection you allow me to bear you. If I am reproached for impotence in this attempt to draw from the depths of mysticism a book which seeks to give, in the lucid transparency of our beautiful language, the luminous poesy of the Orient, to you the blame! Did you not command this struggle (resembling that of Jacob) by telling me that the most imperfect sketch of this Figure, dreamed of by you, as it has been by me since childhood, would still be something to you?

Here, then, it is,—that something. Would that this book could belong exclusively to noble spirits, preserved like yours from worldly pettiness by solitude! THEY would know how to give to it the melodious rhythm that it lacks, which might have made it, in the hands of a poet, the glorious epic that France still awaits.

But from me they must accept it as one of those sculptured balustrades, carved by a hand of faith, on which the pilgrims lean, in the choir of some glorious church, to think upon the end of man.

I am, madame, with respect,
Your devoted servant,
De Balzac.

CONTENTS

CHAPTER I

SERAPHITUS

As the eye glances over a map of the coasts of Norway, can the imagination fail to marvel at their fantastic indentations and serrated edges, like a granite lace, against which the surges of the North Sea roar incessantly? Who has not dreamed of the majestic sights to be seen on those beachless shores, of that multitude of creeks and inlets and little bays, no two of them alike, yet all trackless abysses? We may almost fancy that Nature took pleasure in recording by ineffaceable hieroglyphics the symbol of Norwegian life, bestowing on these coasts the conformation of a fish's spine, fishery being the staple commerce of the country, and well-nigh the only means of living of the hardy men who cling like tufts of lichen to the arid cliffs. Here, through fourteen degrees of longitude, barely seven hundred thousand souls maintain existence. Thanks to perils devoid of glory, to year-long snows which clothe the Norway peaks and guard them from profaning foot of traveller, these sublime beauties are virgin still; they will be seen to harmonize with human phenomena, also virgin—at least to poetry—which here took place, the history of which it is our purpose to relate.

If one of these inlets, mere fissures to the eyes of the eiderducks, is wide enough for the sea not to freeze between the prison-walls of rock against which it surges, the country-people call the little bay a "fiord,"—a word which geographers of every nation have adopted into their respective languages. Though a certain resemblance exists among all these fiords, each has its own characteristics. The sea has everywhere forced its way as through a breach, yet the rocks about each fissure are diversely rent, and their tumultuous precipices defy the rules of geometric law. Here the scarp is dentelled like a saw; there the narrow ledges barely allow the snow to lodge or the noble crests of the Northern pines to spread themselves; farther on, some convulsion of Nature may have rounded a coquettish curve into a lovely valley flanked in rising terraces with black-plumed pines. Truly we are tempted to call this land the Switzerland of Ocean.

Midway between Trondhjem and Christiansand lies an inlet called the Strom-fiord. If the Strom-fiord is not the loveliest of these rocky landscapes, it has the merit of displaying the terrestrial grandeurs of Norway, and of enshrining the scenes of a history that is indeed celestial.

The general outline of the Strom-fiord seems at first sight to be that of a funnel washed out by the sea. The passage which the waves have forced present to the eye an image of the eternal struggle between old Ocean and the granite rock,—two creations of equal power, one through inertia, the other by ceaseless motion. Reefs of fantastic shape run out on either side, and bar the way of ships and forbid their entrance. The intrepid sons of Norway cross these reefs on foot, springing from rock to rock, undismayed at the abyss—a hundred fathoms deep and only six feet wide—which yawns beneath them. Here a tottering block of gneiss falling athwart two rocks gives an uncertain footway; there the hunters or the fishermen, carrying their loads, have flung the stems of fir-trees in guise of bridges, to join the projecting reefs, around and beneath which the surges roar incessantly. This dangerous entrance to the little bay bears obliquely to the right with a serpentine movement, and there encounters a mountain rising some twenty-five hundred feet above sea-level, the base of which is a vertical palisade of solid rock more than a mile and a half long, the inflexible granite nowhere yielding to clefts or undulations until it reaches a height of two hundred feet above the water. Rushing violently in, the sea is driven back with equal violence by the inert force of the mountain to the opposite shore, gently curved by the spent force of the retreating waves.

The fiord is closed at the upper end by a vast gneiss formation crowned with forests, down which a river plunges in cascades, becomes a torrent when the snows are melting, spreads into a sheet of waters, and then falls with a roar into the bay,—vomiting as it does so the hoary pines and the aged larches washed down from the forests and scarce seen amid the foam. These trees plunge headlong into the fiord and reappear after a time on the surface, clinging together and forming islets which float ashore on the beaches, where the inhabitants of a village on the left bank of the Strom-fiord gather them up, split, broken (though sometimes whole), and always stripped of bark and branches. The mountain which receives at its base the assaults of Ocean, and at its summit the buffeting of the wild North wind, is called the Falberg. Its crest, wrapped at all seasons in a mantle of snow and ice, is the sharpest peak of Norway; its proximity to the pole produces, at the height of eighteen hundred feet, a degree of cold equal to that of the highest mountains of the globe. The summit of this rocky mass, rising sheer from the fiord on one side, slopes gradually downward to the east, where it joins the declivities of the Sieg and forms a series of terraced valleys, the chilly temperature of which allows no growth but that of shrubs and stunted trees.

The upper end of the fiord, where the waters enter it as they come down from the forest, is called the Siegdahlen,—a word which may be held to mean "the shedding of the Sieg,"—the river itself receiving that name. The curving shore opposite to the face of the Falberg is the valley of Jarvis,—a smiling scene overlooked by hills clothed with firs, birch-trees, and larches, mingled with a few oaks and beeches, the richest coloring of all the varied tapestries which Nature in these northern regions spreads upon the surface of her rugged rocks. The eye can readily mark the line where the soil, warmed by the rays of the sun, bears cultivation and shows the native growth of the Norwegian flora. Here the expanse of the fiord is broad enough to allow the sea, dashed back by the Falberg, to spend its expiring force in gentle murmurs upon the lower slope of these hills,—a shore bordered with finest sand, strewn with mica and sparkling pebbles, porphyry, and marbles of a thousand tints, brought from Sweden by the river floods, together with ocean waifs, shells, and flowers of the sea driven in by tempests, whether of the Pole or Tropics.

At the foot of the hills of Jarvis lies a village of some two hundred wooden houses, where an isolated population lives like a swarm of bees in a forest, without increasing or diminishing;

vegetating happily, while wringing their means of living from the breast of a stern Nature. The almost unknown existence of the little hamlet is readily accounted for. Few of its inhabitants were bold enough to risk their lives among the reefs to reach the deep-sea fishing,—the staple industry of Norwegians on the least dangerous portions of their coast. The fish of the fiord were numerous enough to suffice, in part at least, for the sustenance of the inhabitants; the valley pastures provided milk and butter; a certain amount of fruitful, well-tilled soil yielded rye and hemp and vegetables, which necessity taught the people to protect against the severity of the cold and the fleeting but terrible heat of the sun with the shrewd ability which Norwegians display in the two-fold struggle. The difficulty of communication with the outer world, either by land where the roads are impassable, or by sea where none but tiny boats can thread their way through the maritime defiles that guard the entrance to the bay, hinder these people from growing rich by the sale of their timber. It would cost enormous sums to either blast a channel out to sea or construct a way to the interior. The roads from Christiana to Trondhjem all turn toward the Strom-fiord, and cross the Sieg by a bridge some score of miles above its fall into the bay. The country to the north, between Jarvis and Trondhjem, is covered with impenetrable forests, while to the south the Falberg is nearly as much separated from Christiana by inaccessible precipices. The village of Jarvis might perhaps have communicated with the interior of Norway and Sweden by the river Sieg; but to do this and to be thus brought into contact with civilization, the Strom-fiord needed the presence of a man of genius. Such a man did actually appear there,—a poet, a Swede of great religious fervor, who died admiring, even reverencing this region as one of the noblest works of the Creator.

Minds endowed by study with an inward sight, and whose quick perceptions bring before the soul, as though painted on a canvas, the contrasting scenery of this universe, will now apprehend the general features of the Strom-fiord. They alone, perhaps, can thread their way through the tortuous channels of the reef, or flee with the battling waves to the everlasting rebuff of the Falberg whose white peaks mingle with the vaporous clouds of the pearl-gray sky, or watch with delight the curving sheet of waters, or hear the rushing of the Sieg as it hangs for an instant in long fillets and then falls over a picturesque abatis of noble trees toppled confusedly together, sometimes upright, sometimes half-sunken beneath the rocks. It may be that such minds alone can dwell upon the smiling scenes nestling among the lower hills of Jarvis; where the luscious Northern vegetables spring up in families, in myriads, where the white birches bend, graceful as maidens, where colonnades of beeches rear their boles mossy with the growth of centuries, where shades of green contrast, and white clouds float amid the blackness of the distant pines, and tracts of many-tinted crimson and purple shrubs are shaded endlessly; in short, where blend all colors, all perfumes of a flora whose wonders are still ignored. Widen the boundaries of this limited ampitheatre, spring upward to the clouds, lose yourself among the rocks where the seals are lying and even then your thought cannot compass the wealth of beauty nor the poetry of this Norwegian coast. Can your thought be as vast as the ocean that bounds it? as weird as the fantastic forms drawn by these forests, these clouds, these shadows, these changeful lights?

Do you see above the meadows on that lowest slope which undulates around the higher hills of Jarvis two or three hundred houses roofed with "noever," a sort of thatch made of birch-bark,—frail houses, long and low, looking like silk-worms on a mulberry-leaf tossed hither by the winds? Above these humble, peaceful dwellings stands the church, built with a simplicity in keeping with the poverty of the villagers. A graveyard surrounds the chancel, and a little farther on you see the parsonage. Higher up, on a projection of the mountain is a dwelling-house, the only one of stone; for which reason the inhabitants of the village call it "the Swedish Castle." In fact, a wealthy Swede settled in Jarvis about thirty years before this history begins, and did his best to ameliorate its condition. This little house, certainly not a castle, built with the intention of leading the inhabitants to build others like it, was noticeable for its solidity and for the wall that inclosed it, a rare thing in Norway where, notwithstanding the abundance of stone, wood alone is used for all fences, even those of fields. This Swedish house, thus protected against the climate, stood on rising ground in the centre of an immense courtyard. The windows were sheltered by those projecting pent-house roofs supported by squared trunks of trees which give so patriarchal an air to Northern dwellings. From beneath them the eye could see the savage nudity of the Falberg, or compare the infinitude of the open sea with the tiny drop of water in the foaming fiord; the ear could hear the flowing of the Sieg, whose white sheet far away looked motionless as it fell into its granite cup edged for miles around with glaciers,—in short, from this vantage ground the whole landscape whereon our simple yet superhuman drama was about to be enacted could be seen and noted.

The winter of 1799-1800 was one of the most severe ever known to Europeans. The Norwegian sea was frozen in all the fiords, where, as a usual thing, the violence of the surf kept the ice from forming. A wind, whose effects were like those of the Spanish levanter, swept the ice of the Strom-fiord, driving the snow to the upper end of the gulf. Seldom indeed could the people of Jarvis see the mirror of frozen waters reflecting the colors of the sky; a wondrous site in the bosom of these mountains when all other aspects of nature are levelled beneath successive sheets of snow, and crests and valleys are alike mere folds of the vast mantle flung by winter across a landscape at once so mournfully dazzling and so monotonous. The falling volume of the Sieg, suddenly frozen, formed an immense arcade beneath which the inhabitants might have crossed under shelter from the blast had any dared to risk themselves inland. But the dangers of every step away from their own surroundings kept even the boldest hunters in their homes, afraid lest the narrow paths along the precipices, the clefts and fissures among the rocks, might be unrecognizable beneath the snow.

Thus it was that no human creature gave life to the white desert where Boreas reigned, his voice alone resounding at distant intervals. The sky, nearly always gray, gave tones of polished steel to the ice of the fiord. Perchance some ancient eider-duck crossed the expanse, trusting to the warm down beneath which dream, in other lands, the luxurious rich, little knowing of the dangers through which their luxury has come to them. Like the Bedouin of the desert who darts alone across the sands of Africa, the bird is neither seen nor heard; the torpid atmosphere, deprived of its electrical conditions, echoes neither the whirr of its wings nor its joyous notes. Besides, what human eye was strong enough to bear the glitter of those pinnacles adorned with sparkling crystals, or the sharp reflections of the snow, iridescent on the summits in the rays of a pallid sun which infrequently appeared, like a dying man seeking to make known that he still lives. Often, when the flocks of gray clouds, driven in squadrons athwart the mountains and among the tree-tops, hid the sky with their triple veils Earth, lacking the celestial lights, lit herself by herself.

Here, then, we meet the majesty of Cold, seated eternally at the pole in that regal silence which is the attribute of all absolute monarchy. Every extreme principle carries with it an appearance of negation and the symptoms of death; for is not life the struggle of two forces? Here in this Northern nature nothing lived. One sole power—the unproductive power of ice—reigned unchallenged. The roar of the open sea no longer reached the deaf, dumb inlet, where during one short season of the year Nature made haste to produce the slender harvests necessary for the food of the patient people. A few tall pine-trees lifted their black pyramids garlanded with snow, and the form of their long branches and depending shoots completed the mourning garments of those solemn heights.

Each household gathered in its chimney-corner, in houses carefully closed from the outer air, and well supplied with biscuit, melted butter, dried fish, and other provisions laid in for the seven-months winter. The very smoke of these dwellings was hardly seen, half-hidden as they were beneath the snow, against the weight of which they were protected by long planks reaching from the roof and fastened at some distance to solid blocks on the ground, forming a covered way around each building.

During these terrible winter months the women spun and dyed the woollen stuffs and the linen fabrics with which they clothed their families, while the men read, or fell into those endless meditations which have given birth to so many profound theories, to the mystic dreams of the North, to its beliefs, to its studies (so full and so complete in one science, at least, sounded as with a plummet), to its manners and its morals, half-monastic, which force the soul to react and feed upon itself and make the Norwegian peasant a being apart among the peoples of Europe.

Such was the condition of the Strom-fiord in the first year of the nineteenth century and about the middle of the month of May.

On a morning when the sun burst forth upon this landscape, lighting the fires of the ephemeral diamonds produced by crystallizations of the snow and ice, two beings crossed the fiord and flew along the base of the Falberg, rising thence from ledge to ledge toward the summit. What were they? human creatures, or two arrows? They might have been taken for eider-ducks sailing in consort before the wind. Not the boldest hunter nor the most superstitious fisherman would have attributed to human beings the power to move safely along the slender lines traced beneath the snow by the granite ledges, where yet this couple glided with the terrifying dexterity of somnambulists who, forgetting their own weight and the dangers of the slightest deviation, hurry along a ridge-pole and keep their equilibrium by the power of some mysterious force.

"Stop me, Seraphitus," said a pale young girl, "and let me breathe. I look at you, you only, while scaling these walls of the gulf; otherwise, what would become of me? I am such a feeble creature. Do I tire you?"

"No," said the being on whose arm she leaned. "But let us go on, Minna; the place where we are is not firm enough to stand on."

Once more the snow creaked sharply beneath the long boards fastened to their feet, and soon they reached the upper terrace of the first ledge, clearly defined upon the flank of the precipice. The person whom Minna had addressed as Seraphitus threw his weight upon his right heel, arresting the plank—six and a half feet long and narrow as the foot of a child—which was fastened to his boot by a double thong of leather. This plank, two inches thick, was covered with reindeer skin, which bristled against the snow when the foot was raised, and served to stop the wearer. Seraphitus drew in his left foot, furnished with another "skee," which was only two feet long, turned swiftly where he stood, caught his timid companion in his arms, lifted her in spite of the long boards on her feet, and placed her on a projecting rock from which he brushed the snow with his pelisse.

"You are safe there, Minna; you can tremble at your ease."

"We are a third of the way up the Ice-Cap," she said, looking at the peak to which she gave the popular name by which it is known in Norway; "I can hardly believe it."

Too much out of breath to say more, she smiled at Seraphitus, who, without answering, laid his hand upon her heart and listened to its sounding throbs, rapid as those of a frightened bird.

"It often beats as fast when I run," she said.

Seraphitus inclined his head with a gesture that was neither coldness nor indifference, and yet, despite the grace which made the movement almost tender, it none the less bespoke a certain negation, which in a woman would have seemed an exquisite coquetry. Seraphitus clasped the young girl in his arms. Minna accepted the caress as an answer to her words, continuing to gaze at him. As he raised his head, and threw back with impatient gesture the golden masses of his hair to free his brow, he saw an expression of joy in the eyes of his companion.

"Yes, Minna," he said in a voice whose paternal accents were charming from the lips of a being who was still adolescent, "Keep your eyes on me; do not look below you."

"Why not?" she asked.

"You wish to know why? then look!"

Minna glanced quickly at her feet and cried out suddenly like a child who sees a tiger. The awful sensation of abysses seized her; one glance sufficed to communicate its contagion. The fiord, eager for food, bewildered her with its loud voice ringing in her ears, interposing between herself and life as though to devour her more surely. From the crown of her head to her feet and along her spine an icy shudder ran; then suddenly intolerable heat suffused her nerves, beat in her veins and overpowered her extremities with electric shocks like those of the torpedo. Too feeble to resist, she felt herself drawn by a mysterious power to the depths below, wherein she fancied that she saw some monster belching its venom, a monster whose magnetic eyes were charming her, whose open jaws appeared to craunch their prey before they seized it.

"I die, my Seraphitus, loving none but thee," she said, making a mechanical movement to fling herself into the abyss.

Seraphitus breathed softly on her forehead and eyes. Suddenly, like a traveller relaxed after a bath, Minna forgot these keen emotions, already dissipated by that caressing breath which penetrated her body and filled it with balsamic essences as quickly as the breath itself had crossed the air.

"Who art thou?" she said, with a feeling of gentle terror. "Ah, but I know! thou art my life. How canst thou look into that gulf and not die?" she added presently.

Seraphitus left her clinging to the granite rock and placed himself at the edge of the narrow platform on which they stood, whence his eyes plunged to the depths of the fiord, defying its dazzling invitation. His body did not tremble, his brow was white and calm as that of a marble statue,—an abyss facing an abyss.

"Seraphitus! dost thou not love me? come back!" she cried. "Thy danger renews my terror. Who art thou to have such superhuman power at thy age?" she asked as she felt his arms inclosing her once more.

"But, Minna," answered Seraphitus, "you look fearlessly at greater spaces far than that."

Then with raised finger, this strange being pointed upward to the blue dome, which parting clouds left clear above their heads, where stars could be seen in open day by virtue of atmospheric laws as yet unstudied.

"But what a difference!" she answered smiling.

"You are right," he said; "we are born to stretch upward to the skies. Our native land, like the face of a mother, cannot terrify her children."

His voice vibrated through the being of his companion, who made no reply.

"Come! let us go on," he said.

The pair darted forward along the narrow paths traced back and forth upon the mountain, skimming from terrace to terrace, from line to line, with the rapidity of a barb, that bird of the desert.

Presently they reached an open space, carpeted with turf and moss and flowers, where no foot had ever trod.

"Oh, the pretty saeter!" cried Minna, giving to the upland meadow its Norwegian name. "But how comes it here, at such a height?"

"Vegetation ceases here, it is true," said Seraphitus. "These few plants and flowers are due to that sheltering rock which protects the meadow from the polar winds. Put that tuft in your bosom, Minna," he added, gathering a flower, — "that balmy creation which no eye has ever seen; keep the solitary matchless flower in memory of this one matchless morning of your life. You will find no other guide to lead you again to this saeter."

So saying, he gave her the hybrid plant his falcon eye had seen amid the tufts of gentian acaulis and saxifrages, — a marvel, brought to bloom by the breath of angels. With girlish eagerness Minna seized the tufted plant of transparent green, vivid as emerald, which was formed of little leaves rolled trumpet-wise, brown at the smaller end but changing tint by tint to their delicately notched edges, which were green. These leaves were so tightly pressed together that they seemed to blend and form a mat or cluster of rosettes. Here and there from this green ground rose pure white stars edged with a line of gold, and from their throats came crimson anthers but no pistils. A fragrance, blended of roses and of orange blossoms, yet ethereal and fugitive, gave something as it were celestial to that mysterious flower, which Seraphitus sadly contemplated, as though it uttered plaintive thoughts which he alone could understand. But to Minna this mysterious phenomenon seemed a mere caprice of nature giving to stone the freshness, softness, and perfume of plants.

"Why do you call it matchless? can it not reproduce itself?" she asked, looking at Seraphitus, who colored and turned away.

"Let us sit down," he said presently; "look below you, Minna. See! At this height you will have no fear. The abyss is so far beneath us that we no longer have a sense of its depths; it acquires the perspective uniformity of ocean, the vagueness of clouds, the soft coloring of the sky. See, the ice of the fiord is a turquoise, the dark pine forests are mere threads of brown; for us all abysses should be thus adorned."

Seraphitus said the words with that fervor of tone and gesture seen and known only by those who have ascended the highest mountains of the globe,—a fervor so involuntarily acquired that the haughtiest of men is forced to regard his guide as a brother, forgetting his own superior station till he descends to the valleys and the abodes of his kind. Seraphitus unfastened the skees from Minna's feet, kneeling before her. The girl did not notice him, so absorbed was she in the marvellous view now offered of her native land, whose rocky outlines could here be seen at a glance. She felt, with deep emotion, the solemn permanence of those frozen summits, to which words could give no adequate utterance.

"We have not come here by human power alone," she said, clasping her hands. "But perhaps I dream."

"You think that facts the causes of which you cannot perceive are supernatural," replied her companion.

"Your replies," she said, "always bear the stamp of some deep thought. When I am near you I understand all things without an effort. Ah, I am free!"

"If so, you will not need your skees," he answered.

"Oh!" she said; "I who would fain unfasten yours and kiss your feet!"

"Keep such words for Wilfrid," said Seraphitus, gently.

"Wilfrid!" cried Minna angrily; then, softening as she glanced at her companion's face and trying, but in vain, to take his hand, she added, "You are never angry, never; you are so hopelessly perfect in all things."

"From which you conclude that I am unfeeling."

Minna was startled at this lucid interpretation of her thought.

"You prove to me, at any rate, that we understand each other," she said, with the grace of a loving woman.

Seraphitus softly shook his head and looked sadly and gently at her.

"You, who know all things," said Minna, "tell me why it is that the timidity I felt below is over now that I have mounted higher.

Why do I dare to look at you for the first time face to face, while lower down I scarcely dared to give a furtive glance?"

"Perhaps because we are withdrawn from the pettiness of earth," he answered, unfastening his pelisse.

"Never, never have I seen you so beautiful!" cried Minna, sitting down on a mossy rock and losing herself in contemplation of the being who had now guided her to a part of the peak hitherto supposed to be inaccessible.

Never, in truth, had Seraphitus shone with so bright a radiance,—the only word which can render the illumination of his face and the aspect of his whole person. Was this splendor due to the lustre which the pure air of mountains and the reflections of the snow give to the complexion? Was it produced by the inward impulse which excites the body at the instant when exertion is arrested? Did it come from the sudden contrast between the glory of the sun and the darkness of the clouds, from whose shadow the charming couple had just emerged? Perhaps to all these causes we may add the effect of a phenomenon, one of the noblest which human nature has to offer. If some able physiologist had studied this being (who, judging by the pride on his brow and the lightning in his eyes seemed a youth of about seventeen years of age), and if the student had sought for the springs of that beaming life beneath the whitest skin that ever the North bestowed upon her offspring, he would undoubtedly have believed either in some phosphoric fluid of the nerves shining beneath the cuticle, or in the constant presence of an inward luminary, whose rays issued through the being of Seraphitus like a light through an alabaster vase. Soft and slender as were his hands, ungloved to remove his companion's snow-boots, they seemed possessed of a strength equal to that which the Creator gave to the diaphanous tentacles of the crab. The fire darting from his vivid glance seemed to struggle with the beams of the sun, not to take but to give them light. His body, slim and delicate as that of a woman, gave evidence of one of those natures which are feeble apparently, but whose strength equals their will, rendering them at times powerful. Of medium height, Seraphitus appeared to grow in stature as he turned fully round and seemed about to spring upward. His hair, curled by a fairy's hand and waving to the breeze, increased the illusion produced by this aerial attitude; yet his bearing, wholly without conscious effort, was the result far more of a moral phenomenon than of a corporal habit.

Minna's imagination seconded this illusion, under the dominion of which all persons would assuredly have fallen,—an illusion which gave to Seraphitus the appearance of a vision dreamed of in happy sleep. No known type conveys an image of that form so majestically made to Minna, but which to the eyes of a man would have eclipsed in womanly grace the fairest of Raphael's creations. That painter of heaven has ever put a tranquil joy, a loving sweetness, into the lines of his angelic conceptions; but what soul, unless it contemplated Seraphitus himself, could have conceived the ineffable emotions imprinted on his face? Who would have divined, even in the dreams of artists, where all things become possible, the shadow cast by some mysterious awe upon that brow, shining with intellect, which seemed to question Heaven and to pity Earth? The head hovered awhile disdainfully, as some majestic bird whose cries reverberate on the atmosphere, then bowed itself resignedly, like the turtledove uttering soft notes of tenderness in the depths of the silent woods. His complexion was of marvellous whiteness, which brought out vividly the coral lips, the brown eyebrows, and the silken lashes, the only colors that trenched upon the paleness of that face, whose perfect regularity did not detract from the grandeur of the sentiments expressed in it; nay, thought and emotion were reflected there, without hindrance or violence, with the majestic and natural gravity which we delight in attributing to superior beings. That face of purest marble expressed in all things strength and peace.

Minna rose to take the hand of Seraphitus, hoping thus to draw him to her, and to lay on that seductive brow a kiss given more from admiration than from love; but a glance at the young man's eyes, which pierced her as a ray of sunlight penetrates a prism, paralyzed the young girl. She felt, but without comprehending, a gulf between them; then she turned away her head and wept. Suddenly a strong hand seized her by the waist, and a soft voice said to her: "Come!" She obeyed, resting her head, suddenly revived, upon the heart of her companion, who, regulating his step to hers with gentle and attentive conformity, led her to a spot whence they could see the radiant glories of the polar Nature.

"Before I look, before I listen to you, tell me, Seraphitus, why you repulse me. Have I displeased you? and how? tell me! I want nothing for myself; I would that all my earthly goods were yours, for the riches of my heart are yours already. I would that light came to my eyes only though your eyes just as my thought is born of your thought. I should not then fear to offend you, for I should give you back the echoes of your soul, the words of your heart, day by day,—as we render to God the meditations with which his spirit nourishes our minds. I would be thine alone."

"Minna, a constant desire is that which shapes our future. Hope on! But if you would be pure in heart mingle the idea of the All-Powerful with your affections here below; then you will love all creatures, and your heart will rise to heights indeed."

"I will do all you tell me," she answered, lifting her eyes to his with a timid movement.

"I cannot be your companion," said Seraphitus sadly.

He seemed to repress some thoughts, then stretched his arms towards Christiana, just visible like a speck on the horizon and said:—

"Look!"

"We are very small," she said.

"Yes, but we become great through feeling and through intellect," answered Seraphitus. "With us, and us alone, Minna, begins the knowledge of things; the little that we learn of the laws of the visible world enables us to apprehend the immensity of the worlds invisible. I know not if the time has come to speak thus to you, but I would, ah, I would communicate to you the flame of my hopes! Perhaps we may one day be together in the world where Love never dies."

"Why not here and now?" she said, murmuring.

"Nothing is stable here," he said, disdainfully. "The passing joys of earthly love are gleams which reveal to certain souls the coming of joys more durable; just as the discovery of a single law of nature leads certain privileged beings to a conception of the system of the universe. Our fleeting happiness here below is the forerunning proof of another and a perfect happiness, just as the earth, a fragment of the world, attests the universe. We cannot measure the vast orbit of the Divine thought of which we are but an atom as small as God is great; but we can feel its vastness, we can kneel, adore, and wait. Men ever mislead themselves in science by not perceiving that all things on their globe are related and co-ordinated to the general evolution, to a constant movement and production which bring with them, necessarily, both advancement and an End. Man himself is not a finished creation; if he were, God would not Be."

"How is it that in thy short life thou hast found the time to learn so many things?" said the young girl.

"I remember," he replied.

"Thou art nobler than all else I see."

"We are the noblest of God's greatest works. Has He not given us the faculty of reflecting on Nature; of gathering it within us by thought; of making it a footstool and stepping-stone from and by which to rise to Him? We love according to the greater or the lesser portion of heaven our souls contain. But do not be unjust, Minna; behold the magnificence spread before you. Ocean expands at your feet like a carpet; the mountains resemble ampitheatres; heaven's ether is above them like the arching folds of a stage curtain. Here we may breathe the thoughts of God, as it were like a perfume. See! the angry billows which engulf the ships laden with men seem to us, where we are, mere bubbles; and if we raise our eyes and look above, all there is blue. Behold that diadem of stars! Here the tints of earthly impressions disappear; standing on this nature rarefied by space do you not feel within you something deeper far than mind, grander than enthusiasm, of greater energy than will? Are you not conscious of emotions whose interpretation is no longer in us? Do you not feel your pinions? Let us pray."

Seraphitus knelt down and crossed his hands upon his breast, while Minna fell, weeping, on her knees. Thus they remained for a time, while the azure dome above their heads grew larger and strong rays of light enveloped them without their knowledge.

"Why dost thou not weep when I weep?" said Minna, in a broken voice.

"They who are all spirit do not weep," replied Seraphitus rising; "Why should I weep? I see no longer human wretchedness. Here, Good appears in all its majesty. There, beneath us, I hear the supplications and the wailings of that harp of sorrows which vibrates in the hands of captive souls. Here, I listen to the choir of harps harmonious. There, below, is hope, the glorious inception of faith; but here is faith—it reigns, hope realized!"

"You will never love me; I am too imperfect; you disdain me," said the young girl.

"Minna, the violet hidden at the feet of the oak whispers to itself: 'The sun does not love me; he comes not.' The sun says: 'If my rays shine upon her she will perish, poor flower.' Friend of the flower, he sends his beams through the oak leaves, he veils, he tempers them, and thus they color the petals of his beloved. I have not veils enough, I fear lest you see me too closely; you would tremble if you knew me better. Listen: I have no taste for earthly fruits. Your joys, I know them all too well, and, like the sated emperors of pagan Rome, I have reached disgust of all things; I have received the gift of vision. Leave me! abandon me!" he murmured, sorrowfully.

Seraphitus turned and seated himself on a projecting rock, dropping his head upon his breast.

"Why do you drive me to despair?" said Minna.

"Go, go!" cried Seraphitus, "I have nothing that you want of me. Your love is too earthly for my love. Why do you not love Wilfrid? Wilfrid is a man, tested by passions; he would clasp you in his vigorous arms and make you feel a hand both broad and strong. His hair is black, his eyes are full of human thoughts, his heart pours lava in every word he utters; he could kill you with caresses. Let him be your beloved, your husband! Yes, thine be Wilfrid!"

Minna wept aloud.

"Dare you say that you do not love him?" he went on, in a voice which pierced her like a dagger.

"Have mercy, have mercy, my Seraphitus!"

"Love him, poor child of Earth to which thy destiny has indissolubly bound thee," said the strange being, beckoning Minna by a gesture, and forcing her to the edge of the saeter, whence he pointed downward to a scene that might well inspire a young girl full of enthusiasm with the fancy that she stood above this earth.

"I longed for a companion to the kingdom of Light; I wished to show you that morsel of mud, I find you bound to it. Farewell. Remain on earth; enjoy through the senses; obey your nature; turn pale with pallid men; blush with women; sport with children; pray with the guilty; raise your eyes to heaven when sorrows overtake you; tremble, hope, throb in all your pulses; you will have a companion; you can laugh and weep, and give and receive. I,—I am an exile, far from heaven; a monster, far from earth. I live of myself and by myself. I feel by the spirit; I breathe through my brow; I see by thought; I die of impatience and of longing. No one here below can fulfil my desires or calm my griefs. I have forgotten how to weep. I am alone. I resign myself, and I wait."

Seraphitus looked at the flowery mound on which he had seated Minna; then he turned and faced the frowning heights, whose pinnacles were wrapped in clouds; to them he cast, unspoken, the remainder of his thoughts.

"Minna, do you hear those delightful strains?" he said after a pause, with the voice of a dove, for the eagle's cry was hushed; "it is like the music of those Eolian harps your poets hang in forests and on the mountains. Do you see the shadowy figures passing among the clouds, the winged feet of those who are making ready the gifts of heaven? They bring refreshment to the soul; the skies are about to open and shed the flowers of spring upon the earth. See, a gleam is darting from the pole. Let us fly, let us fly! It is time we go!"

In a moment their skees were refastened, and the pair descended the Falberg by the steep slopes which join the mountain to the valleys of the Sieg. Miraculous perception guided their course, or, to speak more properly, their flight. When fissures covered with snow intercepted them, Seraphitus caught Minna in his arms and darted with rapid motion, lightly as a bird, over the crumbling causeways of the abyss. Sometimes, while propelling his companion, he deviated to the right or left to avoid a precipice, a tree, a projecting rock, which he seemed to see beneath the snow, as an old sailor, familiar with the ocean, discerns the hidden reefs by the color, the trend, or the eddying of the water. When they reached the paths of the Siegdahlen, where they could fearlessly follow a straight line to regain the ice of the fiord, Seraphitus stopped Minna.

"You have nothing to say to me?" he asked.

"I thought you would rather think alone," she answered respectfully.

"Let us hasten, Minette; it is almost night," he said.

Minna quivered as she heard the voice, now so changed, of her guide,—a pure voice, like that of a young girl, which dissolved the fantastic dream through which she had been passing. Seraphitus seemed to be laying aside his male force and the too keen intellect that flames from his eyes. Presently the charming pair glided across the fiord and reached the snow-field which divides the shore from the first range of houses; then, hurrying forward as daylight faded, they sprang up the hill toward the parsonage, as though they were mounting the steps of a great staircase.

"My father must be anxious," said Minna.

"No," answered Seraphitus.

As he spoke the couple reached the porch of the humble dwelling where Monsieur Becker, the pastor of Jarvis, sat reading while awaiting his daughter for the evening meal.

"Dear Monsieur Becker," said Seraphitus, "I have brought Minna back to you safe and sound."

"Thank you, mademoiselle," said the old man, laying his spectacles on his book; "you must be very tired."

"Oh, no," said Minna, and as she spoke she felt the soft breath of her companion on her brow.

"Dear heart, will you come day after to-morrow evening and take tea with me?"

"Gladly, dear."

"Monsieur Becker, you will bring her, will you not?"

"Yes, mademoiselle."

Seraphitus inclined his head with a pretty gesture, and bowed to the old pastor as he left the house. A few moments later he reached the great courtyard of the Swedish villa. An old servant, over eighty years of age, appeared in the portico bearing a lantern. Seraphitus slipped off his snow-shoes with the graceful dexterity of a woman, then darting into the salon he fell exhausted and motionless on a wide divan covered with furs.

"What will you take?" asked the old man, lighting the immensely tall wax-candles that are used in Norway.

"Nothing, David, I am too weary."

Seraphitus unfastened his pelisse lined with sable, threw it over him, and fell asleep. The old servant stood for several minutes gazing with loving eyes at the singular being before him, whose sex it would have been difficult for any one at that moment to determine. Wrapped as he was in a formless garment, which resembled equally a woman's robe and a man's mantle, it was impossible not to fancy that the slender feet which hung at the side of the couch were those of a woman, and equally impossible not to note how the forehead and the outlines of the head gave evidence of power brought to its highest pitch.

"She suffers, and she will not tell me," thought the old man. "She is dying, like a flower wilted by the burning sun."

And the old man wept.

CHAPTER II

SERAPHITA

Later in the evening David re-entered the salon.

"I know who it is you have come to announce," said Seraphita in a sleepy voice. "Wilfrid may enter."

Hearing these words a man suddenly presented himself, crossed the room and sat down beside her.

"My dear Seraphita, are you ill?" he said. "You look paler than usual."

She turned slowly towards him, tossing back her hair like a pretty woman whose aching head leaves her no strength even for complaint.

"I was foolish enough to cross the fiord with Minna," she said. "We ascended the Falberg."

"Do you mean to kill yourself?" he said with a lover's terror.

"No, my good Wilfrid; I took the greatest care of your Minna."

Wilfrid struck his hand violently on a table, rose hastily, and made several steps towards the door with an exclamation full of pain; then he returned and seemed about to remonstrate.

"Why this disturbance if you think me ill?" she said.

"Forgive me, have mercy!" he cried, kneeling beside her. "Speak to me harshly if you will; exact all that the cruel fancies of a woman lead you to imagine I least can bear; but oh, my beloved, do not doubt my love. You take Minna like an axe to hew me down. Have mercy!"

"Why do you say these things, my friend, when you know that they are useless?" she replied, with a look which grew in the end so soft that Wilfrid ceased to behold her eyes, but saw in their place a fluid light, the shimmer of which was like the last vibrations of an Italian song.

"Ah! no man dies of anguish!" he murmured.

"You are suffering?" she said in a voice whose intonations

produced upon his heart the same effect as that of her look. "Would I could help you!"

"Love me as I love you."

"Poor Minna!" she replied.

"Why am I unarmed!" exclaimed Wilfrid, violently.

"You are out of temper," said Seraphita, smiling. "Come, have I not spoken to you like those Parisian women whose loves you tell of?"

Wilfrid sat down, crossed his arms, and looked gloomily at Seraphita. "I forgive you," he said; "for you know not what you do."

"You mistake," she replied; "every woman from the days of Eve does good and evil knowingly."

"I believe it," he said.

"I am sure of it, Wilfrid. Our instinct is precisely that which makes us perfect. What you men learn, we feel."

"Why, then, do you not feel how much I love you?"

"Because you do not love me."

"Good God!"

"If you did, would you complain of your own sufferings?"

"You are terrible to-night, Seraphita. You are a demon."

"No, but I am gifted with the faculty of comprehending, and it is awful. Wilfrid, sorrow is a lamp which illumines life."

"Why did you ascend the Falberg?"

"Minna will tell you. I am too weary to talk. You must talk to me,—you who know so much, who have learned all things and forgotten nothing; you who have passed through every social test. Talk to me, amuse me, I am listening."

"What can I tell you that you do not know? Besides, the request is ironical. You allow yourself no intercourse with social life; you trample on its conventions, its laws, its customs, sentiments, and sciences; you reduce them all to the proportions such things take when viewed by you beyond this universe."

"Therefore you see, my friend, that I am not a woman. You do wrong to love me. What! am I to leave the ethereal regions of my pretended strength, make myself humbly small, cringe like the hapless female of all species, that you may lift me up? and then, when I, helpless and broken, ask you for help, when I need your arm, you will repulse me! No, we can never come to terms."

"You are more maliciously unkind to-night than I have ever known you."

"Unkind!" she said, with a look which seemed to blend all feelings into one celestial emotion, "no, I am ill, I suffer, that is all. Leave me, my friend; it is your manly right. We women should ever please you, entertain you, be gay in your presence and have no whims save those that amuse you. Come, what shall I do for you, friend? Shall I sing, shall I dance, though weariness deprives me of the use of voice and limbs?—Ah! gentlemen, be we on our deathbeds, we yet must smile to please you; you call that, methinks, your right. Poor women! I pity them. Tell me, you who abandon them when they grow old, is it because they have neither hearts nor souls? Wilfrid, I am a hundred years old; leave me! leave me! go to Minna!"

"Oh, my eternal love!"

"Do you know the meaning of eternity? Be silent, Wilfrid. You desire me, but you do not love me. Tell me, do I not seem to you like those coquettish Parisian women?"

"Certainly I no longer find you the pure celestial maiden I first saw in the church of Jarvis."

At these words Seraphita passed her hands across her brow, and when she removed them Wilfrid was amazed at the saintly expression that overspread her face.

"You are right, my friend," she said; "I do wrong whenever I set my feet upon your earth."

"Oh, Seraphita, be my star! stay where you can ever bless me with that clear light!"

As he spoke, he stretched forth his hand to take that of the young girl, but she withdrew it, neither disdainfully nor in anger. Wilfrid rose abruptly and walked to the window that she might not see the tears that rose to his eyes.

"Why do you weep?" she said. "You are not a child, Wilfrid. Come back to me. I wish it. You are annoyed if I show just displeasure. You see that I am fatigued and ill, yet you force me to

23

think and speak, and listen to persuasions and ideas that weary me. If you had any real perception of my nature, you would have made some music, you would have lulled my feelings—but no, you love me for yourself and not for myself."

The storm which convulsed the young man's heart calmed down at these words. He slowly approached her, letting his eyes take in the seductive creature who lay exhausted before him, her head resting in her hand and her elbow on the couch.

"You think that I do not love you," she resumed. "You are mistaken. Listen to me, Wilfrid. You are beginning to know much; you have suffered much. Let me explain your thoughts to you. You wished to take my hand just now"; she rose to a sitting posture, and her graceful motions seemed to emit light. "When a young girl allows her hand to be taken it is as though she made a promise, is it not? and ought she not to fulfil it? You well know that I cannot be yours. Two sentiments divide and inspire the love of all the women of the earth. Either they devote themselves to suffering, degraded, and criminal beings whom they desire to console, uplift, redeem; or they give themselves to superior men, sublime and strong, whom they adore and seek to comprehend, and by whom they are often annihilated. You have been degraded, though now you are purified by the fires of repentance, and to-day you are once more noble; but I know myself too feeble to be your equal, and too religious to bow before any power but that On High. I may refer thus to your life, my friend, for we are in the North, among the clouds, where all things are abstractions."

"You stab me, Seraphita, when you speak like this. It wounds me to hear you apply the dreadful knowledge with which you strip from all things human the properties that time and space and form have given them, and consider them mathematically in the abstract, as geometry treats substances from which it extracts solidity."

"Well, I will respect your wishes, Wilfrid. Let the subject drop. Tell me what you think of this bearskin rug which my poor David has spread out."

"It is very handsome."

"Did you ever see me wear this 'doucha greka'?"

She pointed to a pelisse made of cashmere and lined with the skin of the black fox,—the name she gave it signifying "warm to the soul."

"Do you believe that any sovereign has a fur that can equal it?" she asked.

"It is worthy of her who wears it."

"And whom you think beautiful?"

"Human words do not apply to her. Heart to heart is the only language I can use."

"Wilfrid, you are kind to soothe my griefs with such sweet words—which you have said to others."

"Farewell!"

"Stay. I love both you and Minna, believe me. To me you two are as one being. United thus you can be my brother or, if you will, my sister. Marry her; let me see you both happy before I leave this world of trial and of pain. My God! the simplest of women obtain what they ask of a lover; they whisper 'Hush!' and he is silent; 'Die' and he dies; 'Love me afar' and he stays at a distance, like courtiers before a king! All I desire is to see you happy, and you refuse me! Am I then powerless?—Wilfrid, listen, come nearer to me. Yes, I should grieve to see you marry Minna but—when I am here no longer, then—promise me to marry her; heaven destined you for each other."

"I listen to you with fascination, Seraphita. Your words are incomprehensible, but they charm me. What is it you mean to say?"

"You are right; I forget to be foolish,—to be the poor creature whose weaknesses gratify you. I torment you, Wilfrid. You came to these Northern lands for rest, you, worn-out by the impetuous struggle of genius unrecognized, you, weary with the patient toils of science, you, who well-nigh dyed your hands in crime and wore the fetters of human justice—"

Wilfrid dropped speechless on the carpet. Seraphita breathed softly on his forehead, and in a moment he fell asleep at her feet.

"Sleep! rest!" she said, rising.

She passed her hands over Wilfrid's brow; then the following sentences escaped her lips, one by one,—all different in tone and accent, but all melodious, full of a Goodness that seemed to emanate from her head in vaporous waves, like the gleams the goddess chastely lays upon Endymion sleeping.

"I cannot show myself such as I am to thee, dear Wilfrid,—to thee who art strong.

"The hour is come; the hour when the effulgent lights of the future cast their reflections backward on the soul; the hour when the soul awakes into freedom.

"Now am I permitted to tell thee how I love thee. Dost thou not see the nature of my love, a love without self-interest; a sentiment full of thee, thee only; a love which follows thee into the future to light that future for thee—for it is the one True Light. Canst thou now conceive with what ardor I would have thee leave this life which weighs thee down, and behold thee nearer than thou art to that world where Love is never-failing? Can it be aught but suffering to love for one life only? Hast thou not felt a thirst for the eternal love? Dost thou not feel the bliss to which a creature rises when, with twin-soul, it loves the Being who betrays not love, Him before whom we kneel in adoration?

"Would I had wings to cover thee, Wilfrid; power to give thee strength to enter now into that world where all the purest joys of purest earthly attachments are but shadows in the Light that shines, unceasing, to illumine and rejoice all hearts.

"Forgive a friendly soul for showing thee the picture of thy sins, in the charitable hope of soothing the sharp pangs of thy remorse. Listen to the pardoning choir; refresh thy soul in the dawn now rising for thee beyond the night of death. Yes, thy life, thy true life is there!

"May my words now reach thee clothed in the glorious forms of dreams; may they deck themselves with images glowing and radiant as they hover round you. Rise, rise, to the height where men can see themselves distinctly, pressed together though they be like grains of sand upon a sea-shore. Humanity rolls out like a many-colored ribbon. See the diverse shades of that flower of the celestial gardens. Behold the beings who lack intelligence, those who begin to receive it, those who have passed through trials, those who love, those who follow wisdom and aspire to the regions of Light!

"Canst thou comprehend, through this thought made visible,

the destiny of humanity?—whence it came, whither to goeth? Continue steadfast in the Path. Reaching the end of thy journey thou shalt hear the clarions of omnipotence sounding the cries of victory in chords of which a single one would shake the earth, but which are lost in the spaces of a world that hath neither east nor west.

"Canst thou comprehend, my poor beloved Tried-one, that unless the torpor and the veils of sleep had wrapped thee, such sights would rend and bear away thy mind as the whirlwinds rend and carry into space the feeble sails, depriving thee forever of thy reason? Dost thou understand that the Soul itself, raised to its utmost power can scarcely endure in dreams the burning communications of the Spirit?

"Speed thy way through the luminous spheres; behold, admire, hasten! Flying thus thou canst pause or advance without weariness. Like other men, thou wouldst fain be plunged forever in these spheres of light and perfume where now thou art, free of thy swooning body, and where thy thought alone has utterance. Fly! enjoy for a fleeting moment the wings thou shalt surely win when Love has grown so perfect in thee that thou hast no senses left; when thy whole being is all mind, all love. The higher thy flight the less canst thou see the abysses. There are none in heaven. Look at the friend who speaks to thee; she who holds thee above this earth in which are all abysses. Look, behold, contemplate me yet a moment longer, for never again wilt thou see me, save imperfectly as the pale twilight of this world may show me to thee."

Seraphita stood erect, her head with floating hair inclining gently forward, in that aerial attitude which great painters give to messengers from heaven; the folds of her raiment fell with the same unspeakable grace which holds an artist—the man who translates all things into sentiment—before the exquisite well-known lines of Polyhymnia's veil. Then she stretched forth her hand. Wilfrid rose. When he looked at Seraphita she was lying on the bear's-skin, her head resting on her hand, her face calm, her eyes brilliant. Wilfrid gazed at her silently; but his face betrayed a deferential fear in its almost timid expression.

"Yes, dear," he said at last, as though he were answering some question; "we are separated by worlds. I resign myself; I can only adore you. But what will become of me, poor and alone!"

"Wilfrid, you have Minna."

He shook his head.

"Do not be so disdainful; woman understands all things through love; what she does not understand she feels; what she does not feel she sees; when she neither sees, nor feels, nor understands, this angel of earth divines to protect you, and hides her protection beneath the grace of love."

"Seraphita, am I worthy to belong to a woman?"

"Ah, now," she said, smiling, "you are suddenly very modest; is it a snare? A woman is always so touched to see her weakness glorified. Well, come and take tea with me the day after to-morrow evening; good Monsieur Becker will be here, and Minna, the purest and most artless creature I have known on earth. Leave me now, my friend; I need to make long prayers and expiate my sins."

"You, can you commit sin?"

"Poor friend! if we abuse our power, is not that the sin of pride? I have been very proud to-day. Now leave me, till to-morrow."

"Till to-morrow," said Wilfrid faintly, casting a long glance at the being of whom he desired to carry with him an ineffaceable memory.

Though he wished to go far away, he was held, as it were, outside the house for some moments, watching the light which shone from all the windows of the Swedish dwelling.

"What is the matter with me?" he asked himself. "No, she is not a mere creature, but a whole creation. Of her world, even through veils and clouds, I have caught echoes like the memory of sufferings healed, like the dazzling vertigo of dreams in which we hear the plaints of generations mingling with the harmonies of some higher sphere where all is Light and all is Love. Am I awake? Do I still sleep? Are these the eyes before which the luminous space retreated further and further indefinitely while the eyes followed it? The night is cold, yet my head is on fire. I will go to the parsonage. With the pastor and his daughter I shall recover the balance of my mind."

But still he did not leave the spot whence his eyes could plunge into Seraphita's salon. The mysterious creature seemed to him the radiating centre of a luminous circle which formed an atmosphere about her wider than that of other beings; whoever entered it felt the compelling influence of, as it were, a vortex of dazzling light and all consuming thoughts. Forced to struggle against this inexplicable power, Wilfrid only prevailed after strong efforts; but when he reached and passed the inclosing wall of the courtyard, he regained his freedom of will, walked rapidly towards the parsonage, and was soon beneath the high wooden arch which formed a sort of peristyle to Monsieur Becker's dwelling. He opened the first door, against which the wind had driven the snow, and knocked on the inner one, saying:—

"Will you let me spend the evening with you, Monsieur Becker?"

"Yes," cried two voices, mingling their intonations.

Entering the parlor, Wilfrid returned by degrees to real life. He bowed affectionately to Minna, shook hands with Monsieur Becker, and looked about at the picture of a home which calmed the convulsions of his physical nature, in which a phenomenon was taking place analogous to that which sometimes seizes upon men who have given themselves up to protracted contemplations. If some strong thought bears upward on phantasmal wing a man of learning or a poet, isolates him from the external circumstances which environ him here below, and leads him forward through illimitable regions where vast arrays of facts become abstractions, where the greatest works of Nature are but images, then woe betide him if a sudden noise strikes sharply on his senses and calls his errant soul back to its prison-house of flesh and bones. The shock of the reunion of these two powers, body and mind,—one of which partakes of the unseen qualities of a thunderbolt, while the other shares with sentient nature that soft resistant force which deifies destruction,—this shock, this struggle, or, rather let us say, this painful meeting and co-mingling, gives rise to frightful sufferings. The body receives back the flame that consumes it; the flame has once more grasped its prey. This fusion, however, does not take place without convulsions, explosions, tortures; analogous and visible signs of which may be seen in chemistry, when two antagonistic substances which science has united separate.

For the last few days whenever Wilfrid entered Seraphita's presence his body seemed to fall away from him into nothingness. With a single glance this strange being led him in spirit through the spheres where meditation leads the learned man, prayer the pious heart, where vision transports the artist, and sleep the souls of men,—each and all have their own path to the Height, their own guide to reach it, their own individual sufferings in the dire return. In that sphere alone all veils are rent away, and the revelation, the awful flaming certainty of an unknown world, of which the soul brings back mere fragments to this lower sphere, stands revealed. To Wilfrid one hour passed with Seraphita was like the sought-for dreams of Theriakis, in which each knot of nerves becomes the centre of a radiating delight. But he left her bruised and wearied as some young girl endeavoring to keep step with a giant.

The cold air, with its stinging flagellations, had begun to still the nervous tremors which followed the reunion of his two natures, so powerfully disunited for a time; he was drawn towards the parsonage, then towards Minna, by the sight of the every-day home life for which he thirsted as the wandering European thirsts for his native land when nostalgia seizes him amid the fairy scenes of Orient that have seduced his senses. More weary than he had ever yet been, Wilfrid dropped into a chair and looked about him for a time, like a man who awakens from sleep. Monsieur Becker and his daughter accustomed, perhaps, to the apparent eccentricity of their guest, continued the employments in which they were engaged.

The parlor was ornamented with a collection of the shells and insects of Norway. These curiosities, admirably arranged on a background of the yellow pine which panelled the room, formed, as it were, a rich tapestry to which the fumes of tobacco had imparted a mellow tone. At the further end of the room, opposite to the door, was an immense wrought-iron stove, carefully polished by the serving-woman till it shone like burnished steel. Seated in a large tapestried armchair near the stove, before a table, with his feet in a species of muff, Monsieur Becker was reading a folio volume which was propped against a pile of other books as on a desk. At his left

stood a jug of beer and a glass, at his right burned a smoky lamp
fed by some species of fish-oil. The pastor seemed about sixty years
of age. His face belonged to a type often painted by Rembrandt; the
same small bright eyes, set in wrinkles and surmounted by thick
gray eyebrows; the same white hair escaping in snowy flakes from
a black velvet cap; the same broad, bald brow, and a contour of face
which the ample chin made almost square; and lastly, the same
calm tranquillity, which, to an observer, denoted the possession of
some inward power, be it the supremacy bestowed by money, or
the magisterial influence of the burgomaster, or the consciousness
of art, or the cubic force of blissful ignorance. This fine old man,
whose stout body proclaimed his vigorous health, was wrapped in
a dressing-gown of rough gray cloth plainly bound. Between his
lips was a meerschaum pipe, from which, at regular intervals, he
blew the smoke, following with abstracted vision its fantastic
wreathings,—his mind employed, no doubt, in assimilating
through some meditative process the thoughts of the author whose
works he was studying.

On the other side of the stove and near a door which
communicated with the kitchen Minna was indistinctly visible in
the haze of the good man's smoke, to which she was apparently
accustomed. Beside her on a little table were the implements of
household work, a pile of napkins, and another of socks waiting to
be mended, also a lamp like that which shone on the white page of
the book in which the pastor was absorbed. Her fresh young face,
with its delicate outline, expressed an infinite purity which
harmonized with the candor of the white brow and the clear blue
eyes. She sat erect, turning slightly toward the lamp for better light,
unconsciously showing as she did so the beauty of her waist and
bust. She was already dressed for the night in a long robe of white
cotton; a cambric cap, without other ornament than a frill of the
same, confined her hair. Though evidently plunged in some inward
meditation, she counted without a mistake the threads of her
napkins or the meshes of her socks. Sitting thus, she presented the
most complete image, the truest type, of the woman destined for
terrestrial labor, whose glance may piece the clouds of the

sanctuary while her thought, humble and charitable, keeps her ever on the level of man.

Wilfrid had flung himself into a chair between the two tables and was contemplating with a species of intoxication this picture full of harmony, to which the clouds of smoke did no despite. The single window which lighted the parlor during the fine weather was now carefully closed. An old tapestry, used for a curtain and fastened to a stick, hung before it in heavy folds. Nothing in the room was picturesque, nothing brilliant; everything denoted rigorous simplicity, true heartiness, the ease of unconventional nature, and the habits of a domestic life which knew neither cares nor troubles. Many a dwelling is like a dream, the sparkle of passing pleasure seems to hide some ruin beneath the cold smile of luxury; but this parlor, sublime in reality, harmonious in tone, diffused the patriarchal ideas of a full and self-contained existence. The silence was unbroken save by the movements of the servant in the kitchen engaged in preparing the supper, and by the sizzling of the dried fish which she was frying in salt butter according to the custom of the country.

"Will you smoke a pipe?" said the pastor, seizing a moment when he thought that Wilfrid might listen to him.

"Thank you, no, dear Monsieur Becker," replied the visitor.

"You seem to suffer more to-day than usual," said Minna, struck by the feeble tones of the stranger's voice.

"I am always so when I leave the chateau."

Minna quivered.

"A strange being lives there, Monsieur Becker," he continued after a pause. "For the six months that I have been in this village I have never yet dared to question you about her, and even now I do violence to my feelings in speaking of her. I began by keenly regretting that my journey in this country was arrested by the winter weather and that I was forced to remain here. But during the last two months chains have been forged and riveted which bind me irrevocably to Jarvis, till now I fear to end my days here. You know how I first met Seraphita, what impression her look and voice made upon me, and how at last I was admitted to her home where she receives no one. From the very first day I have longed to ask you the history of this mysterious being. On that day began, for me, a series of enchantments."

"Enchantments!" cried the pastor shaking the ashes of his pipe into an earthen-ware dish full of sand, "are there enchantments in these days?"

"You, who are carefully studying at this moment that volume of the 'Incantations' of Jean Wier, will surely understand the explanation of my sensations if I try to give it to you," replied Wilfrid. "If we study Nature attentively in its great evolutions as in its minutest works, we cannot fail to recognize the possibility of enchantment—giving to that word its exact significance. Man does not create forces; he employs the only force that exists and which includes all others namely Motion, the breath incomprehensible of the sovereign Maker of the universe. Species are too distinctly separated for the human hand to mingle them. The only miracle of which man is capable is done through the conjunction of two antagonistic substances. Gunpowder for instance is germane to a thunderbolt. As to calling forth a creation, and a sudden one, all creation demands time, and time neither recedes nor advances at the word of command. So, in the world without us, plastic nature obeys laws the order and exercise of which cannot be interfered with by the hand of man. But after fulfilling, as it were, the function of Matter, it would be unreasonable not to recognize within us the existence of a gigantic power, the effects of which are so incommensurable that the known generations of men have never yet been able to classify them. I do not speak of man's faculty of abstraction, of constraining Nature to confine itself within the Word,—a gigantic act on which the common mind reflects as little as it does on the nature of Motion, but which, nevertheless, has led the Indian theosophists to explain creation by a word to which they give an inverse power. The smallest atom of their subsistence, namely, the grain of rice, from which a creation issues and in which alternately creation again is held, presented to their minds so perfect an image of the creative word, and of the abstractive word, that to them it was easy to apply the same system to the creation of worlds. The majority of men content themselves with the grain of rice sown in the first chapter of all the Geneses. Saint John, when he said the Word was God only complicated the difficulty. But the fructification, germination, and efflorescence of our ideas is of little consequence if we compare that property, shared by many men, with the wholly individual faculty of communicating to that property, by some mysterious concentration, forces that are more or less active, of carrying it up to a third, a ninth, or a twenty-seventh power, of making it thus fasten upon the masses and obtain magical results by condensing the processes of nature.

"What I mean by enchantments," continued Wilfrid after a moment's pause, "are those stupendous actions taking place between two membranes in the tissue of the brain. We find in the unexplorable nature of the Spiritual World certain beings armed with these wondrous faculties, comparable only to the terrible power of certain gases in the physical world, beings who combine with other beings, penetrate them as active agents, and produce upon them witchcrafts, charms, against which these helpless slaves are wholly defenceless; they are, in fact, enchanted, brought under subjection, reduced to a condition of dreadful vassalage. Such mysterious beings overpower others with the sceptre and the glory of a superior nature,—acting upon them at times like the torpedo which electrifies or paralyzes the fisherman, at other times like a dose of phosphorous which stimulates life and accelerates its propulsion; or again, like opium, which puts to sleep corporeal nature, disengages the spirit from every bond, enables it to float above the world and shows this earth to the spiritual eye as through a prism, extracting from it the food most needed; or, yet again, like catalepsy, which deadens all faculties for the sake of one only vision. Miracles, enchantments, incantations, witchcrafts, spells, and charms, in short, all those acts improperly termed supernatural, are only possible and can only be explained by the despotism with which some spirit compels us to feel the effects of a mysterious optic which increases, or diminishes, or exalts creation, moves within us as it pleases, deforms or embellishes all things to our eyes, tears us from heaven, or drags us to hell,—two terms by which men agree to express the two extremes of joy and misery.

"These phenomena are within us, not without us," Wilfrid went on. "The being whom we call Seraphita seems to me one of those rare and terrible spirits to whom power is given to bind men, to crush nature, to enter into participation of the occult power of God. The course of her enchantments over me began on that first day, when silence as to her was imposed upon me against my will. Each time that I have wished to question you it seemed as though I were about to reveal a secret of which I ought to be the incorruptible guardian. Whenever I have tried to speak, a burning seal has been laid upon my lips, and I myself have become the involuntary minister of these mysteries. You see me here to-night, for the hundredth time, bruised, defeated, broken, after leaving the hallucinating sphere which surrounds that young girl, so gentle, so fragile to both of you, but to me the cruellest of magicians! Yes, to me she is like a sorcerer holding in her right hand the invisible wand that moves the globe, and in her left the thunderbolt that rends asunder all things at her will. No longer can I look upon her brow; the light of it is insupportable. I skirt the borders of the abyss of madness too closely to be longer silent. I must speak. I seize this moment, when courage comes to me, to resist the power which drags me onward without inquiring whether or not I have the force to follow. Who is she? Did you know her young? What of her birth? Had she father and mother, or was she born of the conjunction of ice and sun? She burns and yet she freeze; she shows herself and then withdraws; she attracts me and repulses me; she brings me life, she gives me death; I love her and yet I hate her! I cannot live thus; let me be wholly in heaven or in hell!"

Holding his refilled pipe in one hand, and in the other the cover which he forgot to replace, Monsieur Becker listened to Wilfrid with a mysterious expression on his face, looking occasionally at his daughter, who seemed to understand the man's language as in harmony with the strange being who inspired it. Wilfrid was splendid to behold at this moment,—like Hamlet listening to the ghost of his father as it rises for him alone in the midst of the living.

"This is certainly the language of a man in love," said the good pastor, innocently.

"In love!" cried Wilfrid, "yes, to common minds. But, dear Monsieur Becker, no words can express the frenzy which draws me to the feet of that unearthly being."

"Then you do love her?" said Minna, in a tone of reproach.

"Mademoiselle, I feel such extraordinary agitation when I see her, and such deep sadness when I see her no more, that in any other man what I feel would be called love. But that sentiment draws those who feel it ardently together, whereas between her and me a great gulf lies, whose icy coldness penetrates my very being in her presence; though the feeling dies away when I see her no longer. I leave her in despair; I return to her with ardor,—like men of science who seek a secret from Nature only to be baffled, or like the painter who would fain put life upon his canvas and strives with all the resources of his art in the vain attempt."

"Monsieur, all that you say is true," replied the young girl, artlessly.

"How can you know, Minna?" asked the old pastor.

"Ah! my father, had you been with us this morning on the summit of the Falberg, had you seen him praying, you would not ask me that question. You would say, like Monsieur Wilfrid, that he saw his Seraphita for the first time in our temple, 'It is the Spirit of Prayer.'"

These words were followed by a moment's silence.

"Ah, truly!" said Wilfrid, "she has nothing in common with the creatures who grovel upon this earth."

"On the Falberg!" said the old pastor, "how could you get there?"

"I do not know," replied Minna; "the way is like a dream to me, of which no more than a memory remains. Perhaps I should hardly believe that I had been there were it not for this tangible proof."

She drew the flower from her bosom and showed it to them. All three gazed at the pretty saxifrage, which was still fresh, and now shone in the light of the two lamps like a third luminary.

"This is indeed supernatural," said the old man, astounded at the sight of a flower blooming in winter.

"A mystery!" cried Wilfrid, intoxicated with its perfume.

"The flower makes me giddy," said Minna; "I fancy I still hear that voice,—the music of thought; that I still see the light of that look, which is Love."

"I implore you, my dear Monsieur Becker, tell me the history of Seraphita,—enigmatical human flower,—whose image is before us in this mysterious bloom."

"My dear friend," said the old man, emitting a puff of smoke, "to explain the birth of that being it is absolutely necessary that I disperse the clouds which envelop the most obscure of Christian doctrines. It is not easy to make myself clear when speaking of that incomprehensible revelation,—the last effulgence of faith that has shone upon our lump of mud. Do you know Swedenborg?"

"By name only,—of him, of his books, and his religion I know nothing."

"Then I must relate to you the whole chronicle of Swedenborg."

CHAPTER III

SERAPHITA-SERAPHITUS

After a pause, during which the pastor seemed to be gathering his recollections, he continued in the following words:—

"Emanuel Swedenborg was born at Upsala in Sweden, in the month of January, 1688, according to various authors,—in 1689, according to his epitaph. His father was Bishop of Skara. Swedenborg lived eighty-five years; his death occurred in London, March 29, 1772. I use that term to convey the idea of a simple change of state. According to his disciples, Swedenborg was seen at Jarvis and in Paris after that date. Allow me, my dear Monsieur Wilfrid," said Monsieur Becker, making a gesture to prevent all interruption, "I relate these facts without either affirming or denying them. Listen; afterwards you can think and say what you like. I will inform you when I judge, criticise, and discuss these doctrines, so as to keep clearly in view my own intellectual neutrality between HIM and Reason.

"The life of Swedenborg was divided into two parts," continued the pastor. "From 1688 to 1745 Baron Emanuel Swedenborg appeared in the world as a man of vast learning, esteemed and cherished for his virtues, always irreproachable and constantly useful. While fulfilling high public functions in Sweden, he published, between 1709 and 1740, several important works on mineralogy, physics, mathematics, and astronomy, which enlightened the world of learning. He originated a method of building docks suitable for the reception of large vessels, and he wrote many treatises on various important questions, such as the rise of tides, the theory of the magnet and its qualities, the motion and position of the earth and planets, and while Assessor in the Royal College of Mines, on the proper system of working salt mines. He discovered means to construct canal-locks or sluices; and he also discovered and applied the simplest methods of extracting ore and of working metals. In fact he studied no science without advancing it. In youth he learned Hebrew, Greek, and Latin, also the oriental languages, with which he became so familiar that many distinguished scholars consulted him, and he was able to decipher the vestiges of the oldest known books of Scripture, namely: 'The Wars of Jehovah' and 'The Enunciations,' spoken of by Moses (Numbers xxi. 14, 15, 27-30), also by Joshua, Jeremiah, and Samuel,—'The Wars of Jehovah' being the historical part and 'The Enunciations' the prophetical part of the Mosaical Books anterior to Genesis. Swedenborg even affirms that 'the Book of Jasher,' the Book of the Righteous, mentioned by Joshua, was in existence in Eastern Tartary, together with the doctrine of Correspondences. A Frenchman has lately, so they tell me, justified these statements of Swedenborg, by the discovery at Bagdad of several portions of the Bible hitherto unknown to Europe. During the widespread discussion on animal magnetism which took its rise in Paris, and in which most men of Western science took an active part about the year 1785, Monsieur le Marquis de Thome vindicated the memory of Swedenborg by calling attention to certain assertions made by the Commission appointed by the King of France to investigate the subject. These gentlemen declared that no theory of magnetism existed, whereas Swedenborg had studied and promulgated it ever since the year 1720. Monsieur de Thome seizes this opportunity to show the reason why so many men of science relegated Swedenborg to oblivion while they delved into his treasure-house and took his facts to aid their work. 'Some of the most illustrious of these men,' said Monsieur de Thome, alluding to the 'Theory of the Earth' by Buffon, 'have had the meanness to wear the plumage of the noble bird and refuse him all acknowledgment'; and he proved, by masterly quotations drawn from the encyclopaedic works of Swedenborg, that the great prophet had anticipated by over a century the slow march of human science. It suffices to read his philosophical and mineralogical works to be convinced of this. In one passage he is seen as the precursor of modern chemistry by the announcement that the productions of organized nature are decomposable and resolve into two simple principles; also that water, air, and fire are not elements. In another, he goes in a few words to the heart of magnetic mysteries and deprives Mesmer of the honors of a first knowledge of them.

"There," said Monsieur Becker, pointing to a long shelf against the wall between the stove and the window on which were ranged books of all sizes, "behold him! here are seventeen works from his pen, of which one, his 'Philosophical and Mineralogical Works,' published in 1734, is in three folio volumes. These productions, which prove the incontestable knowledge of Swedenborg, were given to me by Monsieur Seraphitus, his cousin and the father of Seraphita.

"In 1740," continued Monsieur Becker, after a slight pause, "Swedenborg fell into a state of absolute silence, from which he emerged to bid farewell to all his earthly occupations; after which his thoughts turned exclusively to the Spiritual Life. He received the first commands of heaven in 1745, and he thus relates the nature of the vocation to which he was called: One evening, in London, after dining with a great appetite, a thick white mist seemed to fill his room. When the vapor dispersed a creature in human form rose from one corner of the apartment, and said in a stern tone, 'Do not eat so much.' He refrained. The next night the same man returned, radiant in light, and said to him, 'I am sent of God, who has chosen you to explain to men the meaning of his Word and his Creation. I will tell you what to write.' The vision lasted but a few moments. The angel was clothed in purple. During that night the eyes of his inner man were opened, and he was forced to look into the heavens, into the world of spirits, and into hell,—three separate spheres; where he encountered persons of his acquaintance who had departed from their human form, some long since, others lately. Thenceforth Swedenborg lived wholly in the spiritual life, remaining in this world only as the messenger of God. His mission was ridiculed by the incredulous, but his conduct was plainly that of a being superior to humanity. In the first place, though limited in means to the bare necessaries of life, he gave away enormous sums, and publicly, in several cities, restored the fortunes of great commercial houses when they were on the brink of failure. No one ever appealed to his generosity who was not immediately satisfied.

A sceptical Englishman, determined to know the truth, followed him to Paris, and relates that there his doors stood always open. One day a servant complained of this apparent negligence, which laid him open to suspicion of thefts that might be committed by others. 'He need feel no anxiety,' said Swedenborg, smiling. 'But I do not wonder at his fear; he cannot see the guardian who protects my door.' In fact, no matter in what country he made his abode he never closed his doors, and nothing was ever stolen from him. At Gottenburg—a town situated some sixty miles from Stockholm—he announced, eight days before the news arrived by courier, the conflagration which ravaged Stockholm, and the exact time at which it took place. The Queen of Sweden wrote to her brother, the King, at Berlin, that one of her ladies-in-waiting, who was ordered by the courts to pay a sum of money which she was certain her husband had paid before his death, went to Swedenborg and begged him to ask her husband where she could find proof of the payment. The following day Swedenborg, having done as the lady requested, pointed out the place where the receipt would be found. He also begged the deceased to appear to his wife, and the latter saw her husband in a dream, wrapped in a dressing-gown which he wore just before his death; and he showed her the paper in the place indicated by Swedenborg, where it had been securely put away. At another time, embarking from London in a vessel commanded by Captain Dixon, he overheard a lady asking if there were plenty of provisions on board. 'We do not want a great quantity,' he said; 'in eight days and two hours we shall reach Stockholm,'—which actually happened. This peculiar state of vision as to the things of the earth—into which Swedenborg could put himself at will, and which astonished those about him—was, nevertheless, but a feeble representative of his faculty of looking into heaven.

"Not the least remarkable of his published visions is that in which he relates his journeys through the Astral Regions; his descriptions cannot fail to astonish the reader, partly through the crudity of their details. A man whose scientific eminence is incontestable, and who united in his own person powers of conception, will, and imagination, would surely have invented better if he had invented at all. The fantastic literature of the East offers nothing that can give an idea of this astounding work, full of the essence of poetry, if it is permissible to compare a work of faith with one of oriental fancy. The transportation of Swedenborg by the Angel who served as guide to this first journey is told with a sublimity which exceeds, by the distance which God has placed betwixt the earth and the sun, the great epics of Klopstock, Milton, Tasso, and Dante. This description, which serves in fact as an introduction to his work on the Astral Regions, has never been published; it is among the oral traditions left by Swedenborg to the three disciples who were nearest to his heart. Monsieur Silverichm has written them down. Monsieur Seraphitus endeavored more than once to talk to me about them; but the recollection of his cousin's words was so burning a memory that he always stopped short at the first sentence and became lost in a revery from which I could not rouse him."

The old pastor sighed as he continued: "The baron told me that the argument by which the Angel proved to Swedenborg that these bodies are not made to wander through space puts all human science out of sight beneath the grandeur of a divine logic. According to the Seer, the inhabitants of Jupiter will not cultivate the sciences, which they call darkness; those of Mercury abhor the expression of ideas by speech, which seems to them too material,— their language is ocular; those of Saturn are continually tempted by evil spirits; those of the Moon are as small as six-year-old children, their voices issue from the abdomen, on which they crawl; those of Venus are gigantic in height, but stupid, and live by robbery,— although a part of this latter planet is inhabited by beings of great sweetness, who live in the love of Good. In short, he describes the customs and morals of all the peoples attached to the different globes, and explains the general meaning of their existence as related to the universe in terms so precise, giving explanations which agree so well with their visible evolutions in the system of the world, that some day, perhaps, scientific men will come to drink of these living waters.

"Here," said Monsieur Becker, taking down a book and

opening it at a mark, "here are the words with which he ended this work:—

"'If any man doubts that I was transported through a vast number of Astral Regions, let him recall my observation of the distances in that other life, namely, that they exist only in relation to the external state of man; now, being transformed within like unto the Angelic Spirits of those Astral Spheres, I was able to understand them.'

"The circumstances to which we of this canton owe the presence among us of Baron Seraphitus, the beloved cousin of Swedenborg, enabled me to know all the events of the extraordinary life of that prophet. He has lately been accused of imposture in certain quarters of Europe, and the public prints reported the following fact based on a letter written by the Chevalier Baylon. Swedenborg, they said, informed by certain senators of a secret correspondence of the late Queen of Sweden with her brother, the Prince of Prussia, revealed his knowledge of the secrets contained in that correspondence to the Queen, making her believe he had obtained this knowledge by supernatural means. A man worthy of all confidence, Monsieur Charles-Leonhard de Stahlhammer, captain in the Royal guard and knight of the Sword, answered the calumny with a convincing letter."

The pastor opened a drawer of his table and looked through a number of papers until he found a gazette which he held out to Wilfrid, asking him to read aloud the following letter:—

Stockholm, May 18, 1788.

I have read with amazement a letter which purports to relate the interview of the famous Swedenborg with Queen Louisa-Ulrika. The circumstances therein stated are wholly false; and I hope the writer will excuse me for showing him by the following faithful narration, which can be proved by the testimony of many distinguished persons then present and still living, how completely he has been deceived.

In 1758, shortly after the death of the Prince of Prussia Swedenborg came to court, where he was in the habit of attending regularly. He had scarcely entered the queen's presence before she said to him: "Well, Mr.

Assessor, have you seen my brother?" Swedenborg answered no, and the queen rejoined: "If you do see him, greet him for me." In saying this she meant no more than a pleasant jest, and had no thought whatever of asking him for information about her brother. Eight days later (not twenty-four as stated, nor was the audience a private one), Swedenborg again came to court, but so early that the queen had not left her apartment called the White Room, where she was conversing with her maids-of-honor and other ladies attached to the court. Swedenborg did not wait until she came forth, but entered the said room and whispered something in her ear. The queen, overcome with amazement, was taken ill, and it was some time before she recovered herself. When she did so she said to those about her: "Only God and my brother knew the thing that he has just spoken of." She admitted that it related to her last correspondence with the prince on a subject which was known to them alone. I cannot explain how Swedenborg came to know the contents of that letter, but I can affirm on my honor, that neither Count H— (as the writer of the article states) nor any other person intercepted, or read, the queen's letters. The senate allowed her to write to her brother in perfect security, considering the correspondence as of no interest to the State. It is evident that the author of the said article is ignorant of the character of Count H—. This honored gentleman, who has done many important services to his country, unites the qualities of a noble heart to gifts of mind, and his great age has not yet weakened these precious possessions. During his whole administration he added the weight of scrupulous integrity to his enlightened policy and openly declared himself the enemy of all secret intrigues and underhand dealings, which he regarded as unworthy means to attain an end. Neither did the writer of that article understand the Assessor Swedenborg. The only weakness of that essentially honest man was a belief in the apparition of spirits; but I knew him for many years, and I can affirm that he was as fully convinced that he met and talked with spirits as I am that I am writing at this moment. As a citizen and as a friend his integrity was absolute; he abhorred deception and led the most exemplary of lives. The version which the Chevalier Baylon gave of these facts is, therefore, entirely without justification; the visit stated to have been made to Swedenborg in the night-time by Count H— and Count T— is hereby contradicted. In conclusion, the writer of the letter may rest assured that I am not a follower of Swedenborg. The love of truth alone impels me to give this faithful account of a fact which has been so often stated with details that are entirely false. I certify to the truth of what I have written by adding my signature.

Charles-Leonhard de Stahlhammer.

"The proofs which Swedenborg gave of his mission to the royal families of Sweden and Prussia were no doubt the foundation of the belief in his doctrines which is prevalent at the two courts," said Monsieur Becker, putting the gazette into the drawer. "However," he continued, "I shall not tell you all the facts of his visible and material life; indeed his habits prevented them from being fully known. He lived a hidden life; not seeking either riches or fame. He was even noted for a sort of repugnance to making proselytes; he opened his mind to few persons, and never showed his external powers of second-sight to any who were not eminent in faith, wisdom, and love. He could recognize at a glance the state of the soul of every person who approached him, and those whom he desired to reach with his inward language he converted into Seers. After the year 1745, his disciples never saw him do a single thing from any human motive. One man alone, a Swedish priest, named Mathesius, set afloat a story that he went mad in London in 1744. But a eulogium on Swedenborg prepared with minute care as to all the known events of his life, was pronounced after his death in 1772 on behalf of the Royal Academy of Sciences in the Hall of the Nobles at Stockholm, by Monsieur Sandels, counsellor of the Board of Mines. A declaration made before the Lord Mayor of London gives the details of his last illness and death, in which he received the ministrations of Monsieur Ferelius a Swedish priest of the highest standing, and pastor of the Swedish Church in London, Mathesius being his assistant. All persons present attested that so far from denying the value of his writings Swedenborg firmly asserted their truth. 'In one hundred years,' Monsieur Ferelius quotes him as saying, 'my doctrine will guide the Church.' He predicted the day and hour of his death. On that day, Sunday, March 29, 1772, hearing the clock strike, he asked what time it was.

45

'Five o'clock' was the answer. 'It is well,' he answered; 'thank you, God bless you.' Ten minutes later he tranquilly departed, breathing a gentle sigh. Simplicity, moderation, and solitude were the features of his life. When he had finished writing any of his books he sailed either for London or for Holland, where he published them, and never spoke of them again. He published in this way twenty-seven different treatises, all written, he said, from the dictation of Angels. Be it true or false, few men have been strong enough to endure the flames of oral illumination.

"There they all are," said Monsieur Becker, pointing to a second shelf on which were some sixty volumes. "The treatises on which the Divine Spirit casts its most vivid gleams are seven in number, namely: 'Heaven and Hell'; 'Angelic Wisdom concerning the Divine Love and the Divine Wisdom'; 'Angelic Wisdom concerning the Divine Providence'; 'The Apocalypse Revealed'; 'Conjugial Love and its Chaste Delights'; 'The True Christian Religion'; and 'An Exposition of the Internal Sense.' Swedenborg's explanation of the Apocalypse begins with these words," said Monsieur Becker, taking down and opening the volume nearest to him: "'Herein I have written nothing of mine own; I speak as I am bidden by the Lord, who said, through the same angel, to John: "Thou shalt not seal the sayings of this Prophecy."' (Revelation xxii. 10.)

"My dear Monsieur Wilfrid," said the old man, looking at his guest, "I often tremble in every limb as I read, during the long winter evenings the awe-inspiring works in which this man declares with perfect artlessness the wonders that are revealed to him. 'I have seen,' he says, 'Heaven and the Angels. The spiritual man sees his spiritual fellows far better than the terrestrial man sees the men of earth. In describing the wonders of heaven and beneath the heavens I obey the Lord's command. Others have the right to believe me or not as they choose. I cannot put them into the state in which God has put me; it is not in my power to enable them to converse with Angels, nor to work miracles within their understanding; they alone can be the instrument of their rise to angelic intercourse. It is now twenty-eight years since I have lived in the Spiritual world with angels, and on earth with men; for it pleased God to open the eyes of my spirit as he did that of Paul, and of Daniel and Elisha.'

"And yet," continued the pastor, thoughtfully, "certain persons have had visions of the spiritual world through the complete detachment which somnambulism produces between their external form and their inner being. 'In this state,' says Swedenborg in his treatise on Angelic Wisdom (No. 257) 'Man may rise into the region of celestial light because, his corporeal senses being abolished, the influence of heaven acts without hindrance on his inner man.' Many persons who do not doubt that Swedenborg received celestial revelations think that his writings are not all the result of divine inspiration. Others insist on absolute adherence to him; while admitting his many obscurities, they believe that the imperfection of earthly language prevented the prophet from clearly revealing those spiritual visions whose clouds disperse to the eyes of those whom faith regenerates; for, to use the words of his greatest disciple, 'Flesh is but an external propagation.' To poets and to writers his presentation of the marvellous is amazing; to Seers it is simply reality. To some Christians his descriptions have seemed scandalous. Certain critics have ridiculed the celestial substance of his temples, his golden palaces, his splendid cities where angels disport themselves; they laugh at his groves of miraculous trees, his gardens where the flowers speak and the air is white, and the mystical stones, the sard, carbuncle, chrysolite, chrysoprase, jacinth, chalcedony, beryl, the Urim and Thummim, are endowed with motion, express celestial truths, and reply by variations of light to questions put to them ('True Christian Religion,' 219). Many noble souls will not admit his spiritual worlds where colors are heard in delightful concert, where language flames and flashes, where the Word is writ in pointed spiral letters ('True Christian Religion,' 278). Even in the North some writers have laughed at the gates of pearl, and the diamonds which stud the floors and walls of his New Jerusalem, where the most ordinary utensils are made of the rarest substances of the globe. 'But,' say his disciples, 'because such things are sparsely scattered on this earth does it follow that they are not abundant in other worlds? On earth they are terrestrial substances, whereas in heaven they assume celestial forms and are in keeping with angels.' In this connection Swedenborg has used the very words of Jesus Christ, who said, 'If I have told you earthly things and ye believe not, how shall ye believe if I tell you of heavenly things?'

"Monsieur," continued the pastor, with an emphatic gesture, "I have read the whole of Swedenborg's works; and I say it with pride, because I have done it and yet retained my reason. In reading him men either miss his meaning or become Seers like him. Though I have evaded both extremes, I have often experienced unheard-of delights, deep emotions, inward joys, which alone can reveal to us the plenitude of truth,—the evidence of celestial Light. All things here below seem small indeed when the soul is lost in the perusal of these Treatises. It is impossible not to be amazed when we think that in the short space of thirty years this man wrote and published, on the truths of the Spiritual World, twenty-five quarto volumes, composed in Latin, of which the shortest has five hundred pages, all of them printed in small type. He left, they say, twenty others in London, bequeathed to his nephew, Monsieur Silverichm, formerly almoner to the King of Sweden. Certainly a man who, between the ages of twenty and sixty, had already exhausted himself in publishing a series of encyclopaedical works, must have received supernatural assistance in composing these later stupendous treatises, at an age, too, when human vigor is on the wane. You will find in these writings thousands of propositions, all numbered, none of which have been refuted. Throughout we see method and precision; the presence of the spirit issuing and flowing down from a single fact,—the existence of angels. His 'True Christian Religion,' which sums up his whole doctrine and is vigorous with light, was conceived and written at the age of eighty-three. In fact, his amazing vigor and omniscience are not denied by any of his critics, not even by his enemies.

"Nevertheless," said Monsieur Becker, slowly, "though I have drunk deep in this torrent of divine light, God has not opened the eyes of my inner being, and I judge these writings by the reason of an unregenerated man. I have often felt that the inspired Swedenborg must have misunderstood the Angels. I have laughed over certain visions which, according to his disciples, I ought to have believed with veneration. I have failed to imagine the spiral writing of the Angels or their golden belts, on which the gold is of great or lesser thickness. If, for example, this statement, 'Some angels are solitary,' affected me powerfully for a time, I was, on reflection, unable to reconcile this solitude with their marriages. I have not understood why the Virgin Mary should continue to wear blue satin garments in heaven. I have even dared to ask myself why those gigantic demons, Enakim and Hephilim, came so frequently to fight the cherubim on the apocalyptic plains of Armageddon; and I cannot explain to my own mind how Satans can argue with Angels. Monsieur le Baron Seraphitus assured me that those details concerned only the angels who live on earth in human form. The visions of the prophet are often blurred with grotesque figures. One of his spiritual tales, or 'Memorable relations,' as he called them, begins thus: 'I see the spirits assembling, they have hats upon their heads.' In another of these Memorabilia he receives from heaven a bit of paper, on which he saw, he says, the hieroglyphics of the primitive peoples, which were composed of curved lines traced from the finger-rings that are worn in heaven. However, perhaps I am wrong; possibly the material absurdities with which his works are strewn have spiritual significations. Otherwise, how shall we account for the growing influence of his religion? His church numbers to-day more than seven hundred thousand believers,—as many in the United States of America as in England, where there are seven thousand Swedenborgians in the city of Manchester alone. Many men of high rank in knowledge and in social position in Germany, in Prussia, and in the Northern kingdoms have publicly adopted the beliefs of Swedenborg; which, I may remark, are more comforting than those of all other Christian communions. I wish I had the power to explain to you clearly in succinct language the leading points of the doctrine on which Swedenborg founded his church; but I fear such a summary, made from recollection, would be necessarily defective. I shall, therefore, allow myself to speak only of those 'Arcana' which concern the birth of Seraphita."

Here Monsieur Becker paused, as though composing his mind to gather up his ideas. Presently he continued, as follows:—

"After establishing mathematically that man lives eternally in spheres of either a lower or a higher grade, Swedenborg applies the term 'Spiritual Angels' to beings who in this world are prepared for heaven, where they become angels. According to him, God has not created angels; none exist who have not been men upon the earth. The earth is the nursery-ground of heaven. The Angels are therefore not Angels as such ('Angelic Wisdom,' 57), they are transformed through their close conjunction with God; which conjunction God never refuses, because the essence of God is not negative, but essentially active. The spiritual angels pass through three natures of love, because man is only regenerated through successive stages ('True Religion'). First, the love of self: the supreme expression of this love is human genius, whose works are worshipped. Next, love of life: this love produces prophets,—great men whom the world accepts as guides and proclaims to be divine. Lastly, love of heaven, and this creates the Spiritual Angel. These angels are, so to speak, the flowers of humanity, which culminates in them and works for that culmination. They must possess either the love of heaven or the wisdom of heaven, but always Love before Wisdom.

"Thus the transformation of the natural man is into Love. To reach this first degree, his previous existences must have passed through Hope and Charity, which prepare him for Faith and Prayer. The ideas acquired by the exercise of these virtues are transmitted to each of the human envelopes within which are hidden the metamorphoses of the inner being; for nothing is separate, each existence is necessary to the other existences. Hope cannot advance without Charity, nor Faith without Prayer; they are the four fronts of a solid square. 'One virtue missing,' he said, 'and the Spiritual Angel is like a broken pearl.' Each of these existences is therefore a circle in which revolves the celestial riches of the inner being. The perfection of the Spiritual Angels comes from this mysterious progression in which nothing is lost of the high qualities that are successfully acquired to attain each glorious incarnation; for at each transformation they cast away unconsciously the flesh and its errors. When the man lives in Love he has shed all evil passions: Hope, Charity, Faith, and Prayer have, in the words of Isaiah, purged the dross of his inner being, which can never more be polluted by earthly affections. Hence the grand saying of Christ quoted by Saint Matthew, 'Lay up for yourselves treasures in Heaven where neither moth nor rust doth corrupt,' and those still grander words: 'If ye were of this world the world would love you, but I have chosen you out of the world; be ye therefore perfect as your Father in heaven is perfect.'

"The second transformation of man is to Wisdom. Wisdom is the understanding of celestial things to which the Spirit is brought by Love. The Spirit of Love has acquired strength, the result of all vanquished terrestrial passions; it loves God blindly. But the Spirit of Wisdom has risen to understanding and knows why it loves. The wings of the one are spread and bear the spirit to God; the wings of the other are held down by the awe that comes of understanding: the spirit knows God. The one longs incessantly to see God and to fly to Him; the other attains to Him and trembles. The union effected between the Spirit of Love and the Spirit of Wisdom carries the human being into a Divine state during which time his soul is woman and his body man, the last human manifestation in which the Spirit conquers Form, or Form still struggles against the Spirit,—for Form, that is, the flesh, is ignorant, rebels, and desires to continue gross. This supreme trial creates untold sufferings seen by Heaven alone,—the agony of Christ in the Garden of Olives.

"After death the first heaven opens to this dual and purified human nature. Therefore it is that man dies in despair while the Spirit dies in ecstasy. Thus, the natural, the state of beings not yet regenerated; the spiritual, the state of those who have become Angelic Spirits, and the divine, the state in which the Angel exists before he breaks from his covering of flesh, are the three degrees of existence through which man enters heaven. One of Swedenborg's thoughts expressed in his own words will explain to you with wonderful clearness the difference between the natural and the spiritual. 'To the minds of men,' he says, 'the Natural passes into the Spiritual; they regard the world under its visible aspects, they perceive it only as it can be realized by their senses. But to the apprehension of Angelic Spirits, the Spiritual passes into the Natural; they regard the world in its inward essence and not in its form.' Thus human sciences are but analyses of form. The man of science as the world goes is purely external like his knowledge; his inner being is only used to preserve his aptitude for the perception of external truths. The Angelic Spirit goes far beyond that; his knowledge is the thought of which human science is but the utterance; he derives that knowledge from the Logos, and learns the law of correspondences by which the world is placed in unison with heaven. The word of God was wholly written by pure Correspondences, and covers an esoteric or spiritual meaning, which according to the science of Correspondences, cannot be understood. 'There exist,' says Swedenborg ('Celestial Doctrine' 26), 'innumerable Arcana within the hidden meaning of the Correspondences. Thus the men who scoff at the books of the Prophets where the Word is enshrined are as densely ignorant as those other men who know nothing of a science and yet ridicule its truths. To know the Correspondences which exist between the things visible and ponderable in the terrestrial world and the things invisible and imponderable in the spiritual world, is to hold heaven within our comprehension. All the objects of the manifold creations having emanated from God necessarily enfold a hidden meaning; according, indeed, to the grand thought of Isaiah, 'The earth is a garment.'

"This mysterious link between Heaven and the smallest atoms of created matter constitutes what Swedenborg calls a Celestial Arcanum, and his treatise on the 'Celestial Arcana' in which he explains the correspondences or significances of the Natural with, and to, the Spiritual, giving, to use the words of Jacob Boehm, the sign and seal of all things, occupies not less than sixteen volumes containing thirty thousand propositions. 'This marvellous knowledge of Correspondences which the goodness of God granted to Swedenborg,' says one of his disciples, 'is the secret of the interest which draws men to his works. According to him, all things are derived from heaven, all things lead back to heaven. His writings are sublime and clear; he speaks in heaven, and earth hears him. Take one of his sentences by itself and a volume could be made of it'; and the disciple quotes the following passages taken from a thousand others that would answer the same purpose.

"'The kingdom of heaven,' says Swedenborg ('Celestial

Arcana'), 'is the kingdom of motives. Action is born in heaven, thence into the world, and, by degrees, to the infinitely remote parts of earth. Terrestrial effects being thus linked to celestial causes, all things are correspondent and significant. Man is the means of union between the Natural and the Spiritual.'

"The Angelic Spirits therefore know the very nature of the Correspondences which link to heaven all earthly things; they know, too, the inner meaning of the prophetic words which foretell their evolutions. Thus to these Spirits everything here below has its significance; the tiniest flower is a thought,—a life which corresponds to certain lineaments of the Great Whole, of which they have a constant intuition. To them Adultery and the excesses spoken of in Scripture and by the Prophets, often garbled by self-styled scholars, mean the state of those souls which in this world persist in tainting themselves with earthly affections, thus compelling their divorce from Heaven. Clouds signify the veil of the Most High. Torches, shew-bread, horses and horsemen, harlots, precious stones, in short, everything named in Scripture, has to them a clear-cut meaning, and reveals the future of terrestrial facts in their relation to Heaven. They penetrate the truths contained in the Revelation of Saint John the divine, which human science has subsequently demonstrated and proved materially; such, for instance, as the following ('big,' said Swedenborg, 'with many human sciences'): 'I saw a new heaven and a new earth, for the first heaven and the first earth were passed away' (Revelation xxi. 1). These Spirits know the supper at which the flesh of kings and the flesh of all men, free and bond, is eaten, to which an Angel standing in the sun has bidden them. They see the winged woman, clothed with the sun, and the mailed man. 'The horse of the Apocalypse,' says Swedenborg, 'is the visible image of human intellect ridden by Death, for it bears within itself the elements of its own destruction.' Moreover, they can distinguish beings concealed under forms which to ignorant eyes would seem fantastic. When a man is disposed to receive the prophetic afflation of Correspondences, it rouses within him a perception of the Word; he comprehends that the creations are transformations only; his intellect is sharpened, a burning thirst takes possession of him which only Heaven can quench. He conceives, according to the greater or lesser perfection of his inner being, the power of the Angelic Spirits; and he advances, led by Desire (the least imperfect state of unregenerated man) towards Hope, the gateway to the world of Spirits, whence he reaches Prayer, which gives him the Key of Heaven.

"What being here below would not desire to render himself worthy of entrance into the sphere of those who live in secret by Love and Wisdom? Here on earth, during their lifetime, such spirits remain pure; they neither see, nor think, nor speak like other men. There are two ways by which perception comes,—one internal, the other external. Man is wholly external, the Angelic Spirit wholly internal. The Spirit goes to the depth of Numbers, possesses a full sense of them, knows their significances. It controls Motion, and by reason of its ubiquity it shares in all things. 'An Angel,' says Swedenborg, 'is ever present to a man when desired' ('Angelic Wisdom'); for the Angel has the gift of detaching himself from his body, and he sees into heaven as the prophets and as Swedenborg himself saw into it. 'In this state,' writes Swedenborg ('True Religion,' 136), 'the spirit of a man may move from one place to another, his body remaining where it is,—a condition in which I lived for over twenty-six years.' It is thus that we should interpret all Biblical statements which begin, 'The Spirit led me.' Angelic Wisdom is to human wisdom what the innumerable forces of nature are to its action, which is one. All things live again, and move and have their being in the Spirit, which is in God. Saint Paul expresses this truth when he says, 'In Deo sumus, movemur, et vivimus,'—we live, we act, we are in God.

"Earth offers no hindrance to the Angelic Spirit, just as the Word offers him no obscurity. His approaching divinity enables him to see the thought of God veiled in the Logos, just as, living by his inner being, the Spirit is in communion with the hidden meaning of all things on this earth. Science is the language of the Temporal world, Love is that of the Spiritual world. Thus man takes note of more than he is able to explain, while the Angelic Spirit sees and comprehends. Science depresses man; Love exalts the Angel. Science is still seeking, Love has found. Man judges Nature according to his own relations to her; the Angelic Spirit judges it in its relation to Heaven. In short, all things have a voice for the Spirit. Spirits are in the secret of the harmony of all creations with each other; they comprehend the spirit of sound, the spirit of color, the spirit of vegetable life; they can question the mineral, and the mineral makes answer to their thoughts. What to them are sciences and the treasures of the earth when they grasp all things by the eye at all moments, when the worlds which absorb the minds of so many men are to them but the last step from which they spring to God? Love of heaven, or the Wisdom of heaven, is made manifest to them by a circle of light which surrounds them, and is visible to the Elect. Their innocence, of which that of children is a symbol, possesses, nevertheless, a knowledge which children have not; they are both innocent and learned. 'And,' says Swedenborg, 'the innocence of Heaven makes such an impression upon the soul that those whom it affects keep a rapturous memory of it which lasts them all their lives, as I myself have experienced. It is perhaps sufficient,' he goes on, 'to have only a minimum perception of it to be forever changed, to long to enter Heaven and the sphere of Hope.'

"His doctrine of Marriage can be reduced to the following words: 'The Lord has taken the beauty and the grace of the life of man and bestowed them upon woman. When man is not reunited to this beauty and this grace of his life, he is harsh, sad, and sullen; when he is reunited to them he is joyful and complete.' The Angels are ever at the perfect point of beauty. Marriages are celebrated by wondrous ceremonies. In these unions, which produce no children, man contributes the understanding, woman the will; they become one being, one Flesh here below, and pass to heaven clothed in the celestial form. On this earth, the natural attraction of the sexes towards enjoyment is an Effect which allures, fatigues and disgusts; but in the form celestial the pair, now one in Spirit find within theirself a ceaseless source of joy. Swedenborg was led to see these nuptials of the Spirits, which in the words of Saint Luke (xx. 35) are neither marrying nor giving in marriage, and which inspire none but spiritual pleasures. An Angel offered to make him witness of such a marriage and bore him thither on his wings (the wings are a symbol and not a reality). The Angel clothed him in a wedding garment and when Swedenborg, finding himself thus robed in light, asked why, the answer was: 'For these events, our garments are illuminated; they shine; they are made nuptial.' ('Conjugial Love,' 19, 20, 21.) Then he saw the two Angels, one coming from the South, the other from the East; the Angel of the South was in a chariot drawn by two white horses, with reins of the color and brilliance of the dawn; but lo, when they were near him in the sky, chariot and horses vanished. The Angel of the East, clothed in crimson, and the Angel of the South, in purple, drew together, like breaths, and mingled: one was the Angel of Love, the other the Angel of Wisdom. Swedenborg's guide told him that the two Angels had been linked together on earth by an inward friendship and ever united though separated in life by great distances. Consent, the essence of all good marriage upon earth, is the habitual state of Angels in Heaven. Love is the light of their world. The eternal rapture of Angels comes from the faculty that God communicates to them to render back to Him the joy they feel through Him. This reciprocity of infinitude forms their life. They become infinite by participating of the essence of God, who generates Himself by Himself.

"The immensity of the Heavens where the Angels dwell is such that if man were endowed with sight as rapid as the darting of light from the sun to the earth, and if he gazed throughout eternity, his eyes could not reach the horizon, nor find an end. Light alone can give an idea of the joys of heaven. 'It is,' says Swedenborg ('Angelic Wisdom,' 7, 25, 26, 27), 'a vapor of the virtue of God, a pure emanation of His splendor, beside which our greatest brilliance is obscurity. It can compass all; it can renew all, and is never absorbed: it environs the Angel and unites him to God by infinite joys which multiply infinitely of themselves. This Light destroys whosoever is not prepared to receive it. No one here below, nor yet in Heaven can see God and live. This is the meaning of the saying (Exodus xix. 12, 13, 21-23) "Take heed to yourselves that ye go not up into the mount—lest ye break through unto the Lord to gaze, and many perish." And again (Exodus xxxiv. 29-35), "When Moses came down from Mount Sinai with the two Tables of testimony in his hand, his face shone, so that he put a veil upon it when he spake with the people, lest any of them die." The Transfiguration of Jesus Christ likewise revealed the light surrounding the Messengers from on high and the ineffable joys of the Angels who are forever imbued with it. "His face," says Saint Matthew (xvii. 1-5), "did shine as the sun and his raiment was white as the light—and a bright cloud overshadowed them."'

"When a planet contains only those beings who reject the Lord, when his word is ignored, then the Angelic Spirits are gathered together by the four winds, and God sends forth an Exterminating Angel to change the face of the refractory earth, which in the immensity of this universe is to Him what an unfruitful seed is to Nature. Approaching the globe, this Exterminating Angel, borne by a comet, causes the planet to turn upon its axis, and the lands lately covered by the seas reappear, adorned in freshness and obedient to the laws proclaimed in Genesis; the Word of God is once more powerful on this new earth, which everywhere exhibits the effects of terrestrial waters and celestial flames. The light brought by the Angel from On High, causes the sun to pale. 'Then,' says Isaiah, (xix. 20) 'men will hide in the clefts of the rock and roll themselves in the dust of the earth.' 'They will cry to the mountains' (Revelation), 'Fall on us! and to the seas, Swallow us up! Hide us from the face of Him that sitteth on the throne, and from the wrath of the Lamb!' The Lamb is the great figure and hope of the Angels misjudged and persecuted here below. Christ himself has said, 'Blessed are those who mourn! Blessed are the simple-hearted! Blessed are they that love!'—All Swedenborg is there! Suffer, Believe, Love. To love truly must we not suffer? must we not believe? Love begets Strength, Strength bestows Wisdom, thence Intelligence; for Strength and Wisdom demand Will. To be intelligent, is not that to Know, to Wish, and to Will,—the three attributes of the Angelic Spirit? 'If the universe has a meaning,' Monsieur Saint-Martin said to me when I met him during a journey which he made in Sweden, 'surely this is the one most worthy of God.'

"But, Monsieur," continued the pastor after a thoughtful pause, "of what avail to you are these shreds of thoughts taken here and there from the vast extent of a work of which no true idea can be given except by comparing it to a river of light, to billows of flame? When a man plunges into it he is carried away as by an awful current. Dante's poem seems but a speck to the reader submerged in the almost Biblical verses with which Swedenborg renders palpable the Celestial Worlds, as Beethoven built his palaces of harmony with thousands of notes, as architects have reared cathedrals with millions of stones. We roll in soundless depths, where our minds will not always sustain us. Ah, surely a great and powerful intellect is needed to bring us back, safe and sound, to our own social beliefs.

"Swedenborg," resumed the pastor, "was particularly attached to the Baron de Seraphitz, whose name, according to an old Swedish custom, had taken from time immemorial the Latin termination of 'us.' The baron was an ardent disciple of the Swedish prophet, who had opened the eyes of his Inner-Man and brought him to a life in conformity with the decrees from On-High. He sought for an Angelic Spirit among women; Swedenborg found her for him in a vision. His bride was the daughter of a London shoemaker, in whom, said Swedenborg, the life of Heaven shone, she having passed through all anterior trials. After the death, that is, the transformation of the prophet, the baron came to Jarvis to accomplish his celestial nuptials with the observances of Prayer. As for me, who am not a Seer, I have only known the terrestrial works of this couple. Their lives were those of saints whose virtues are the glory of the Roman Church. They ameliorated the condition of our people; they supplied them all with means in return for work,— little, perhaps, but enough for all their wants. Those who lived with them in constant intercourse never saw them show a sign of anger or impatience; they were constantly beneficent and gentle, full of courtesy and loving-kindness; their marriage was the harmony of two souls indissolubly united. Two eiders winging the same flight, the sound in the echo, the thought in the word,—these, perhaps, are true images of their union. Every one here in Jarvis loved them with an affection which I can compare only to the love of a plant for the sun. The wife was simple in her manners, beautiful in form, lovely in face, with a dignity of bearing like that of august personages. In

1783, being then twenty-six years old, she conceived a child; her pregnancy was to the pair a solemn joy. They prepared to bid the earth farewell; for they told me they should be transformed when their child had passed the state of infancy which needed their fostering care until the strength to exist alone should be given to her.

"Their child was born,—the Seraphita we are now concerned with. From the moment of her conception father and mother lived a still more solitary life than in the past, lifting themselves up to heaven by Prayer. They hoped to see Swedenborg, and faith realized their hope. The day on which Seraphita came into the world Swedenborg appeared in Jarvis, and filled the room of the new-born child with light. I was told that he said, 'The work is accomplished; the Heavens rejoice!' Sounds of unknown melodies were heard throughout the house, seeming to come from the four points of heaven on the wings of the wind. The spirit of Swedenborg led the father forth to the shores of the fiord and there quitted him. Certain inhabitants of Jarvis, having approached Monsieur Seraphitus as he stood on the shore, heard him repeat those blissful words of Scripture: 'How beautiful on the mountains are the feet of Him who is sent of God!'

"I had left the parsonage on my way to baptize the infant and name it, and perform the other duties required by law, when I met the baron returning to the house. 'Your ministrations are superfluous,' he said; 'our child is to be without name on this earth. You must not baptize in the waters of an earthly Church one who has just been immersed in the fires of Heaven. This child will remain a blossom, it will not grow old; you will see it pass away. You exist, but our child has life; you have outward senses, the child has none, its being is always inward.' These words were uttered in so strange and supernatural a voice that I was more affected by them than by the shining of his face, from which light appeared to exude. His appearance realized the phantasmal ideas which we form of inspired beings as we read the prophesies of the Bible. But such effects are not rare among our mountains, where the nitre of perpetual snows produces extraordinary phenomena in the human organization.

"I asked him the cause of his emotion. 'Swedenborg came to us; he has just left me; I have breathed the air of heaven,' he replied. 'Under what form did he appear?' I said. 'Under his earthly form; dressed as he was the last time I saw him in London, at the house of Richard Shearsmith, Coldbath-fields, in July, 1771. He wore his brown frieze coat with steel buttons, his waistcoat buttoned to the throat, a white cravat, and the same magisterial wig rolled and powdered at the sides and raised high in front, showing his vast and luminous brow, in keeping with the noble square face, where all is power and tranquillity. I recognized the large nose with its fiery nostril, the mouth that ever smiled,—angelic mouth from which these words, the pledge of my happiness, have just issued, "We shall meet soon."'

"The conviction that shone on the baron's face forbade all discussion; I listened in silence. His voice had a contagious heat which made my bosom burn within me; his fanaticism stirred my heart as the anger of another makes our nerves vibrate. I followed him in silence to his house, where I saw the nameless child lying mysteriously folded to its mother's breast. The babe heard my step and turned its head toward me; its eyes were not those of an ordinary child. To give you an idea of the impression I received, I must say that already they saw and thought. The childhood of this predestined being was attended by circumstances quite extraordinary in our climate. For nine years our winters were milder and our summers longer than usual. This phenomenon gave rise to several discussions among scientific men; but none of their explanations seemed sufficient to academicians, and the baron smiled when I told him of them. The child was never seen in its nudity as other children are; it was never touched by man or woman, but lived a sacred thing upon the mother's breast, and it never cried. If you question old David he will confirm these facts about his mistress, for whom he feels an adoration like that of Louis IX. for the saint whose name he bore.

"At nine years of age the child began to pray; prayer is her life. You saw her in the church at Christmas, the only day on which she comes there; she is separated from the other worshippers by a visible space. If that space does not exist between herself and men she suffers. That is why she passes nearly all her time alone in the chateau. The events of her life are unknown; she is seldom seen; her days are spent in the state of mystical contemplation which was, so Catholic writers tell us, habitual with the early Christian solitaries, in whom the oral tradition of Christ's own words still remained. Her mind, her soul, her body, all within her is virgin as the snow on those mountains. At ten years of age she was just what you see her now. When she was nine her father and mother expired together, without pain or visible malady, after naming the day and hour at which they would cease to be. Standing at their feet she looked at them with a calm eye, not showing either sadness, or grief, or joy, or curiosity. When we approached to remove the two bodies she said, 'Carry them away!' 'Seraphita,' I said, for so we called her, 'are you not affected by the death of your father and your mother who loved you so much?' 'Dead?' she answered, 'no, they live in me forever—That is nothing,' she pointed without emotion to the bodies they were bearing away. I then saw her for the third time only since her birth. In church it is difficult to distinguish her; she stands near a column which, seen from the pulpit, is in shadow, so that I cannot observe her features.

"Of all the servants of the household there remained after the death of the master and mistress only old David, who, in spite of his eighty-two years, suffices to wait on his mistress. Some of our Jarvis people tell wonderful tales about her. These have a certain weight in a land so essentially conducive to mystery as ours; and I am now studying the treatise on Incantations by Jean Wier and other works relating to demonology, where pretended supernatural events are recorded, hoping to find facts analogous to those which are attributed to her."

"Then you do not believe in her?" said Wilfrid.

"Oh yes, I do," said the pastor, genially, "I think her a very capricious girl; a little spoilt by her parents, who turned her head with the religious ideas I have just revealed to you."

Minna shook her head in a way that gently expressed contradiction.

"Poor girl!" continued the old man, "her parents bequeathed to her that fatal exaltation of soul which misleads mystics and renders them all more or less mad. She subjects herself to fasts which horrify poor David. The good old man is like a sensitive plant which quivers at the slightest breeze, and glows under the first sun-ray. His mistress, whose incomprehensible language has become his, is the breeze and the sun-ray to him; in his eyes her feet are diamonds and her brow is strewn with stars; she walks environed with a white and luminous atmosphere; her voice is accompanied by music; she has the gift of rendering herself invisible. If you ask to see her, he will tell you she has gone to the astral regions. It is difficult to believe such a story, is it not? You know all miracles bear more or less resemblance to the story of the Golden Tooth. We have our golden tooth in Jarvis, that is all. Duncker the fisherman asserts that he has seen her plunge into the fiord and come up in the shape of an eider-duck, at other times walking on the billows of a storm. Fergus, who leads the flocks to the saeters, says that in rainy weather a circle of clear sky can be seen over the Swedish castle; and that the heavens are always blue above Seraphita's head when she is on the mountain. Many women hear the tones of a mighty organ when Seraphita enters the church, and ask their neighbors earnestly if they too do not hear them. But my daughter, for whom during the last two years Seraphita has shown much affection, has never heard this music, and has never perceived the heavenly perfumes which, they say, make the air fragrant about her when she moves. Minna, to be sure, has often on returning from their walks together expressed to me the delight of a young girl in the beauties of our spring-time, in the spicy odors of budding larches and pines and the earliest flowers; but after our long winters what can be more natural than such pleasure? The companionship of this so-called spirit has nothing so very extraordinary in it, has it, my child?"

"The secrets of that spirit are not mine," said Minna. "Near it I know all, away from it I know nothing; near that exquisite life I am no longer myself, far from it I forget all. The time we pass together is a dream which my memory scarcely retains. I may have heard yet not remember the music which the women tell of; in that presence, I may have breathed celestial perfumes, seen the glory of the heavens, and yet be unable to recollect them here."

"What astonishes me most," resumed the pastor, addressing Wilfrid, "is to notice that you suffer from being near her."

"Near her!" exclaimed the stranger, "she has never so much as let me touch her hand. When she saw me for the first time her glance intimidated me; she said: 'You are welcome here, for you were to come.' I fancied that she knew me. I trembled. It is fear that forces me to believe in her."

"With me it is love," said Minna, without a blush.

"Are you making fun of me?" said Monsieur Becker, laughing good-humoredly; "you my daughter, in calling yourself a Spirit of Love, and you, Monsieur Wilfrid, in pretending to be a Spirit of Wisdom?"

He drank a glass of beer and so did not see the singular look which Wilfrid cast upon Minna.

"Jesting apart," resumed the old gentleman, "I have been much astonished to hear that these two mad-caps ascended to the summit of the Falberg; it must be a girlish exaggeration; they probably went to the crest of a ledge. It is impossible to reach the peaks of the Falberg."

"If so, father," said Minna, in an agitated voice, "I must have been under the power of a spirit; for indeed we reached the summit of the Ice-Cap."

"This is really serious," said Monsieur Becker. "Minna is always truthful."

"Monsieur Becker," said Wilfrid, "I swear to you that Seraphita exercises such extraordinary power over me that I know no language in which I can give you the least idea of it. She has revealed to me things known to myself alone."

"Somnambulism!" said the old man. "A great many such effects are related by Jean Wier as phenomena easily explained and formerly observed in Egypt."

"Lend me Swedenborg's theosophical works," said Wilfrid, "and let me plunge into those gulfs of light,—you have given me a thirst for them."

Monsieur Becker took down a volume and gave it to his guest, who instantly began to read it. It was about nine o'clock in the evening. The serving-woman brought in the supper. Minna made tea. The repast over, each turned silently to his or her occupation; the pastor read the Incantations; Wilfrid pursued the spirit of Swedenborg; and the young girl continued to sew, her mind absorbed in recollections. It was a true Norwegian evening— peaceful, studious, and domestic; full of thoughts, flowers blooming beneath the snow. Wilfrid, as he devoured the pages of the prophet, lived by his inner senses only; the pastor, looking up at times from his book, called Minna's attention to the absorption of their guest with an air that was half-serious, half-jesting. To Minna's thoughts the face of Seraphitus smiled upon her as it hovered above the clouds of smoke which enveloped them. The clock struck twelve. Suddenly the outer door was opened violently. Heavy but hurried steps, the steps of a terrified old man, were heard in the narrow vestibule between the two doors; then David burst into the parlor.

"Danger, danger!" he cried. "Come! come, all! The evil spirits are unchained! Fiery mitres are on their heads! Demons, Vertumni, Sirens! they tempt her as Jesus was tempted on the mountain! Come, come! and drive them away."

"Do you not recognize the language of Swedenborg?" said the pastor, laughing, to Wilfrid. "Here it is; pure from the source."

But Wilfrid and Minna were gazing in terror at old David, who, with hair erect, and eyes distraught, his legs trembling and covered with snow, for he had come without snow-shoes, stood swaying from side to side, as if some boisterous wind were shaking him.

"Is he harmed?" cried Minna.

"The devils hope and try to conquer her," replied the old man.

The words made Wilfrid's pulses throb.

"For the last five hours she has stood erect, her eyes raised to heaven and her arms extended; she suffers, she cries to God. I cannot cross the barrier; Hell has posted the Vertumni as sentinels. They have set up an iron wall between her and her old David. She wants me, but what can I do? Oh, help me! help me! Come and pray!"

The old man's despair was terrible to see.

"The Light of God is defending her," he went on, with infectious faith, "but oh! she might yield to violence."

"Silence, David! you are raving. This is a matter to be verified. We will go with you," said the pastor, "and you shall see that there are no Vertumni, nor Satans, nor Sirens, in that house."

"Your father is blind," whispered David to Minna.

Wilfrid, on whom the reading of Swedenborg's first treatise, which he had rapidly gone through, had produced a powerful effect, was already in the corridor putting on his skees; Minna was ready in a few moments, and both left the old men far behind as they darted forward to the Swedish castle.

"Do you hear that cracking sound?" said Wilfrid.

"The ice of the fiord stirs," answered Minna; "the spring is coming."

Wilfrid was silent. When the two reached the courtyard they were conscious that they had neither the faculty nor the strength to enter the house.

"What think you of her?" asked Wilfrid.

"See that radiance!" cried Minna, going towards the window of the salon. "He is there! How beautiful! O my Seraphitus, take me!"

The exclamation was uttered inwardly. She saw Seraphitus standing erect, lightly swathed in an opal-tinted mist that disappeared at a little distance from the body, which seemed almost phosphorescent.

"How beautiful she is!" cried Wilfrid, mentally.

Just then Monsieur Becker arrived, followed by David; he saw his daughter and guest standing before the window; going up to them, he looked into the salon and said quietly, "Well, my good David, she is only saying her prayers."

"Ah, but try to enter, Monsieur."

"Why disturb those who pray?" answered the pastor.

At this instant the moon, rising above the Falberg, cast its rays upon the window. All three turned round, attracted by this natural effect which made them quiver; when they turned back to again look at Seraphita she had disappeared.

"How strange!" exclaimed Wilfrid.

"I hear delightful sounds," said Minna.

"Well," said the pastor, "it is all plain enough; she is going to bed."

David had entered the house. The others took their way back in silence; none of them interpreted the vision in the same manner,—Monsieur Becker doubted, Minna adored, Wilfrid longed.

Wilfrid was a man about thirty-six years of age. His figure, though broadly developed, was not wanting in symmetry. Like most men who distinguish themselves above their fellows, he was of medium height; his chest and shoulders were broad, and his neck short,—a characteristic of those whose hearts are near their heads; his hair was black, thick, and fine; his eyes, of a yellow brown, had, as it were, a solar brilliancy, which proclaimed with what avidity his nature aspired to Light. Though these strong and virile features were defective through the absence of an inward peace,—granted only to a life without storms or conflicts,—they plainly showed the inexhaustible resources of impetuous senses and the appetites of instinct; just as every motion revealed the perfection of the man's physical apparatus, the flexibility of his senses, and their fidelity when brought into play. This man might contend with savages, and hear, as they do, the tread of enemies in distant forests; he could follow a scent in the air, a trail on the ground, or see on the horizon the signal of a friend. His sleep was light, like that of all creatures who will not allow themselves to be surprised. His body came quickly into harmony with the climate of any country where his tempestuous life conducted him. Art and science would have admired his organization in the light of a human model. Everything about him was symmetrical and well-balanced,—action and heart, intelligence and will. At first sight he might be classed among purely instinctive beings, who give themselves blindly up to the material wants of life; but in the very morning of his days he had flung himself into a higher social world, with which his feelings harmonized; study had widened his mind, reflection had sharpened his power of thought, and the sciences had enlarged his understanding. He had studied human laws,—the working of self-interests brought into conflict by the passions, and he seemed to have early familiarized himself with the abstractions on which societies rest. He had pored over books,—those deeds of dead humanity; he had spent whole nights of pleasure in every European capital; he had slept on fields of battle the night before the combat and the night that followed victory. His stormy youth may have flung him on the deck of some corsair and sent him among the contrasting regions of the globe; thus it was that he knew the actions of a living humanity. He knew the present and the past,—a double history; that of to-day, that of other days. Many men have been, like Wilfrid, equally powerful by the Hand, by the Heart, by the Head; like him, the majority have abused their triple power. But though this man still held by certain outward liens to the slimy side of humanity, he belonged also and positively to the sphere where force is intelligent. In spite of the many veils which enveloped his soul, there were certain ineffable symptoms of this fact which were visible to pure spirits, to the eyes of the child whose innocence has known no breath of evil passions, to the eyes of the old man who has lived to regain his purity.

These signs revealed a Cain for whom there was still hope,— one who seemed as though he were seeking absolution from the ends of the earth. Minna suspected the galley-slave of glory in the man; Seraphita recognized him. Both admired and both pitied him. Whence came their prescience? Nothing could be more simple nor yet more extraordinary. As soon as we seek to penetrate the secrets of Nature, where nothing is secret, and where it is only necessary to have the eyes to see, we perceive that the simple produces the marvellous.

"Seraphitus," said Minna one evening a few days after Wilfrid's arrival in Jarvis, "you read the soul of this stranger while I have only vague impressions of it. He chills me or else he excites me; but you seem to know the cause of this cold and of this heat; tell me what it means, for you know all about him."

"Yes, I have seen the causes," said Seraphitus, lowing his large eyelids.

"By what power?" asked the curious Minna.

"I have the gift of Specialism," he answered. "Specialism is an inward sight which can penetrate all things; you will only understand its full meaning through a comparison. In the great cities of Europe where works are produced by which the human

Hand seeks to represent the effects of the moral nature was well as those of the physical nature, there are glorious men who express ideas in marble. The sculptor acts on the stone; he fashions it; he puts a realm of ideas into it. There are statues which the hand of man has endowed with the faculty of representing the noble side of humanity, or the whole evil side; most men see in such marbles a human figure and nothing more; a few other men, a little higher in the scale of being, perceive a fraction of the thoughts expressed in the statue; but the Initiates in the secrets of art are of the same intellect as the sculptor; they see in his work the whole universe of his thought. Such persons are in themselves the principles of art; they bear within them a mirror which reflects nature in her slightest manifestations. Well! so it is with me; I have within me a mirror before which the moral nature, with its causes and effects, appears and is reflected. Entering thus into the consciousness of others I am able to divine both the future and the past. How? do you still ask how? Imagine that the marble statue is the body of a man, a piece of statuary in which we see the emotion, sentiment, passion, vice or crime, virtue or repentance which the creating hand has put into it, and you will then comprehend how it is that I read the soul of this foreigner—though what I have said does not explain the gift of Specialism; for to conceive the nature of that gift we must possess it."

Though Wilfrid belonged to the two first divisions of humanity, the men of force and the men of thought, yet his excesses, his tumultuous life, and his misdeeds had often turned him towards Faith; for doubt has two sides; a side to the light and a side to the darkness. Wilfrid had too closely clasped the world under its forms of Matter and of Mind not to have acquired that thirst for the unknown, that longing to go beyond which lay their grasp upon the men who know, and wish, and will. But neither his knowledge, nor his actions, nor his will, had found direction. He had fled from social life from necessity; as a great criminal seeks the cloister. Remorse, that virtue of weak beings, did not touch him. Remorse is impotence, impotence which sins again. Repentance alone is powerful; it ends all. But in traversing the world, which he made his cloister, Wilfrid had found no balm for his wounds; he saw nothing in nature to which he could attach himself. In him, despair had dried the sources of desire. He was one of those beings who, having gone through all passions and come out victorious, have nothing more to raise in their hot-beds, and who, lacking opportunity to put themselves at the head of their fellow-men to trample under iron heel entire populations, buy, at the price of a horrible martyrdom, the faculty of ruining themselves in some belief,—rocks sublime, which await the touch of a wand that comes not to bring the waters gushing from their far-off spring.

Led by a scheme of his restless, inquiring life to the shores of Norway, the sudden arrival of winter had detained the wanderer at Jarvis. The day on which, for the first time, he saw Seraphita, the whole past of his life faded from his mind. The young girl excited emotions which he had thought could never be revived. The ashes gave forth a lingering flame at the first murmurings of that voice. Who has ever felt himself return to youth and purity after growing cold and numb with age and soiled with impurity? Suddenly, Wilfrid loved as he had never loved; he loved secretly, with faith, with fear, with inward madness. His life was stirred to the very source of his being at the mere thought of seeing Seraphita. As he listened to her he was transported into unknown worlds; he was mute before her, she magnetized him. There, beneath the snows, among the glaciers, bloomed the celestial flower to which his hopes, so long betrayed, aspired; the sight of which awakened ideas of freshness, purity, and faith which grouped about his soul and lifted it to higher regions,—as Angels bear to heaven the Elect in those symbolic pictures inspired by the guardian spirit of a great master. Celestial perfumes softened the granite hardness of the rocky scene; light endowed with speech shed its divine melodies on the path of him who looked to heaven. After emptying the cup of terrestrial love which his teeth had bitten as he drank it, he saw before him the chalice of salvation where the limpid waters sparkled, making thirsty for ineffable delights whoever dare apply his lips burning with a faith so strong that the crystal shall not be shattered.

But Wilfrid now encountered the wall of brass for which he had been seeking up and down the earth. He went impetuously to Seraphita, meaning to express the whole force and bearing of a passion under which he bounded like the fabled horse beneath the iron horseman, firm in his saddle, whom nothing moves while the efforts of the fiery animal only made the rider heavier and more solid. He sought her to relate his life,—to prove the grandeur of his soul by the grandeur of his faults, to show the ruins of his desert. But no sooner had he crossed her threshold, and found himself within the zone of those eyes of scintillating azure, that met no limits forward and left none behind, than he grew calm and submissive, as a lion, springing on his prey in the plains of Africa, receives from the wings of the wind a message of love, and stops his bound. A gulf opened before him, into which his frenzied words fell and disappeared, and from which uprose a voice which changed his being; he became as a child, a child of sixteen, timid and frightened before this maiden with serene brow, this white figure whose inalterable calm was like the cruel impassibility of human justice. The combat between them had never ceased until this evening, when with a glance she brought him down, as a falcon making his dizzy spirals in the air around his prey causes it to fall stupefied to earth, before carrying it to his eyrie.

We may note within ourselves many a long struggle the end of which is one of our own actions,—struggles which are, as it were, the reverse side of humanity. This reverse side belongs to God; the obverse side to men. More than once Seraphita had proved to Wilfrid that she knew this hidden and ever varied side, which is to the majority of men a second being. Often she said to him in her dove-like voice: "Why all this vehemence?" when on his way to her he had sworn she should be his. Wilfrid was, however, strong enough to raise the cry of revolt to which he had given utterance in Monsieur Becker's study. The narrative of the old pastor had calmed him. Sceptical and derisive as he was, he saw belief like a sidereal brilliance dawning on his life. He asked himself if Seraphita were not an exile from the higher spheres seeking the homeward way. The fanciful deifications of all ordinary lovers he could not give to this lily of Norway in whose divinity he believed. Why lived she here beside this fiord? What did she? Questions that received no answer filled his mind. Above all, what was about to happen between them? What fate had brought him there? To him, Seraphita was the motionless marble, light nevertheless as a vapor, which Minna had seen that day poised above the precipices of the Falberg. Could she thus stand on the edge of all gulfs without danger, without a tremor of the arching eyebrows, or a quiver of the light of the eye? If his love was to be without hope, it was not without curiosity.

From the moment when Wilfrid suspected the ethereal nature of the enchantress who had told him the secrets of his life in melodious utterance, he had longed to try to subject her, to keep her to himself, to tear her from the heaven where, perhaps, she was awaited. Earth and Humanity seized their prey; he would imitate them. His pride, the only sentiment through which man can long be exalted, would make him happy in this triumph for the rest of his life. The idea sent the blood boiling through his veins, and his heart swelled. If he did not succeed, he would destroy her,—it is so natural to destroy that which we cannot possess, to deny what we cannot comprehend, to insult that which we envy.

On the morrow, Wilfrid, laden with ideas which the extraordinary events of the previous night naturally awakened in his mind, resolved to question David, and went to find him on the pretext of asking after Seraphita's health. Though Monsieur Becker spoke of the old servant as falling into dotage, Wilfrid relied on his own perspicacity to discover scraps of truth in the torrent of the old man's rambling talk.

David had the immovable, undecided, physiognomy of an octogenarian. Under his white hair lay a forehead lined with wrinkles like the stone courses of a ruined wall; and his face was furrowed like the bed of a dried-up torrent. His life seemed to have retreated wholly to the eyes, where light still shone, though its gleams were obscured by a mistiness which seemed to indicate either an active mental alienation or the stupid stare of drunkenness. His slow and heavy movements betrayed the glacial weight of age, and communicated an icy influence to whoever allowed themselves to look long at him,—for he possessed the magnetic force of torpor. His limited intelligence was only roused by the sight, the hearing, or the recollection of his mistress. She was the soul of this wholly material fragment of an existence. Any one seeing David alone by himself would have thought him a corpse; let Seraphita enter, let her voice be heard, or a mention of her be made, and the dead came forth from his grave and recovered speech and motion. The dry bones were not more truly awakened by the divine breath in the valley of Jehoshaphat, and never was that apocalyptic vision better realized than in this Lazarus issuing from the sepulchre into life at the voice of a young girl. His language, which was always figurative and often incomprehensible, prevented the inhabitants of the village from talking with him; but they respected a mind that deviated so utterly from common ways,—a thing which the masses instinctively admire.

Wilfrid found him in the antechamber, apparently asleep beside the stove. Like a dog who recognizes a friend of the family, the old man raised his eyes, saw the foreigner, and did not stir.

"Where is she?" inquired Wilfrid, sitting down beside him.

David fluttered his fingers in the air as if to express the flight of a bird.

"Does she still suffer?" asked Wilfrid.

"Beings vowed to Heaven are able so to suffer that suffering does not lessen their love; this is the mark of the true faith," answered the old man, solemnly, like an instrument which, on being touched, gives forth an accidental note.

"Who taught you those words?"

"The Spirit."

"What happened to her last night? Did you force your way past the Vertumni standing sentinel? did you evade the Mammons?"

"Yes"; answered David, as though awaking from a dream.

The misty gleam of his eyes melted into a ray that came direct from the soul and made it by degrees brilliant as that of an eagle, as intelligent as that of a poet.

"What did you see?" asked Wilfrid, astonished at this sudden change.

"I saw Species and Shapes; I heard the Spirit of all things; I beheld the revolt of the Evil Ones; I listened to the words of the Good. Seven devils came, and seven archangels descended from on high. The archangels stood apart and looked on through veils. The devils were close by; they shone, they acted. Mammon came on his pearly shell in the shape of a beautiful naked woman; her snowy body dazzled the eye, no human form ever equalled it; and he said, 'I am Pleasure; thou shalt possess me!' Lucifer, prince of serpents, was there in sovereign robes; his Manhood was glorious as the beauty of an angel, and he said, 'Humanity shall be at thy feet!' The Queen of misers,—she who gives back naught that she has ever received,—the Sea, came wrapped in her virent mantle; she opened her bosom, she showed her gems, she brought forth her treasures and offered them; waves of sapphire and of emerald came at her bidding; her hidden wonders stirred, they rose to the surface of her breast, they spoke; the rarest pearl of Ocean spread its iridescent wings and gave voice to its marine melodies, saying, 'Twin daughter of suffering, we are sisters! await me; let us go together; all I need is to become a Woman.' The Bird with the wings of an eagle and the paws of a lion, the head of a woman and the body of a horse, the Animal, fell down before her and licked her feet, and promised seven hundred years of plenty to her best-beloved daughter. Then came the most formidable of all, the Child, weeping at her knees, and saying, 'Wilt thou leave me, feeble and suffering as I am? oh, my mother, stay!' and he played with her, and shed languor on the air, and the Heavens themselves had pity for his wail. The Virgin of pure song brought forth her choirs to relax the soul. The Kings of the East came with their slaves, their armies, and their women; the Wounded asked her for succor, the Sorrowful stretched forth their hands: 'Do not leave us! do not leave us!' they cried. I, too, I cried, 'Do not leave us! we adore thee! stay!' Flowers, bursting from the seed, bathed her in their fragrance which uttered, 'Stay!' The giant Enakim came forth from Jupiter, leading Gold and its friends and all the Spirits of the Astral Regions which are joined with him, and they said, 'We are thine for seven hundred years.' At last came Death on his pale horse, crying, 'I will obey thee!' One and all fell prostrate before her. Could you but have seen them! They covered as it were a vast plain, and they cried aloud to her, 'We have nurtured thee, thou art our child; do not abandon us!' At length Life issued from her Ruby Waters, and said, 'I will not leave thee!' then, finding Seraphita silent, she flamed upon her as the sun, crying out, 'I am light!' 'The light is there!' cried Seraphita, pointing to the clouds where stood the archangels; but she was wearied out; Desire had wrung her nerves, she could only cry, 'My God! my God!' Ah! many an Angelic Spirit, scaling the mountain and nigh to the summit, has set his foot upon a rolling stone which plunged him back into the abyss! All these lost Spirits adored her constancy; they stood around her,—a choir without a song,—weeping and whispering, 'Courage!' At last she conquered; Desire—let loose upon her in every Shape and every Species—was vanquished. She stood in prayer, and when at last her eyes were lifted she saw the feet of Angels circling in the Heavens."

"She saw the feet of Angels?" repeated Wilfrid.

"Yes," said the old man.

"Was it a dream that she told you?" asked Wilfrid.

"A dream as real as your life," answered David; "I was there."

The calm assurance of the old servant affected Wilfrid powerfully. He went away asking himself whether these visions were any less extraordinary than those he had read of in Swedenborg the night before.

"If Spirits exist, they must act," he was saying to himself as he entered the parsonage, where he found Monsieur Becker alone.

"Dear pastor," he said, "Seraphita is connected with us in form only, and even that form is inexplicable. Do not think me a madman or a lover; a profound conviction cannot be argued with. Convert my belief into scientific theories, and let us try to enlighten each other. To-morrow evening we shall both be with her."

"What then?" said Monsieur Becker.

"If her eye ignores space," replied Wilfrid, "if her thought is an intelligent sight which enables her to perceive all things in their essence, and to connect them with the general evolution of the universe, if, in a word, she sees and knows all, let us seat the Pythoness on her tripod, let us force this pitiless eagle by threats to spread its wings! Help me! I breathe a fire which burns my vitals; I must quench it or it will consume me. I have found a prey at last, and it shall be mine!"

"The conquest will be difficult," said the pastor, "because this girl is—"

"Is what?" cried Wilfrid.

"Mad," said the old man.

"I will not dispute her madness, but neither must you dispute her wonderful powers. Dear Monsieur Becker, she has often confounded me with her learning. Has she travelled?"

"From her house to the fiord, no further."

"Never left this place!" exclaimed Wilfrid. "Then she must have read immensely."

"Not a page, not one iota! I am the only person who possesses any books in Jarvis. The works of Swedenborg—the only books that were in the chateau—you see before you. She has never looked into a single one of them."

"Have you tried to talk with her?"

"What good would that do?"

"Does no one live with her in that house?"

"She has no friends but you and Minna, nor any servant except old David."

"It cannot be that she knows nothing of science nor of art."

"Who should teach her?" said the pastor.

"But if she can discuss such matters pertinently, as she has often done with me, what do you make of it?"

"The girl may have acquired through years of silence the faculties enjoyed by Apollonius of Tyana and other pretended sorcerers burned by the Inquisition, which did not choose to admit the fact of second-sight."

"If she can speak Arabic, what would you say to that?"

"The history of medical science gives many authentic instances of girls who have spoken languages entirely unknown to them."

"What can I do?" exclaimed Wilfrid. "She knows of secrets in my past life known only to me."

"I shall be curious if she can tell me thoughts that I have confided to no living person," said Monsieur Becker.

Minna entered the room.

"Well, my daughter, and how is your familiar spirit?"

"He suffers, father," she answered, bowing to Wilfrid. "Human passions, clothed in their false riches, surrounded him all night, and showed him all the glories of the world. But you think these things mere tales."

"Tales as beautiful to those who read them in their brains as the 'Arabian Nights' to common minds," said the pastor, smiling.

"Did not Satan carry our Savior to the pinnacle of the Temple, and show him all the kingdoms of the world?" she said.

"The Evangelists," replied her father, "did not correct their copies very carefully, and several versions are in existence."

"You believe in the reality of these visions?" said Wilfrid to Minna.

"Who can doubt when he relates them."

"He?" demanded Wilfrid. "Who?"

"He who is there," replied Minna, motioning towards the chateau.

"Are you speaking of Seraphita?" he said.

The young girl bent her head, and looked at him with an expression of gentle mischief.

"You too!" exclaimed Wilfrid, "you take pleasure in confounding me. Who and what is she? What do you think of her?"

"What I feel is inexplicable," said Minna, blushing.

"You are all crazy!" cried the pastor.

"Farewell, until to-morrow evening," said Wilfrid.

CHAPTER IV

THE CLOUDS OF THE SANCTUARY

There are pageants in which all the material splendors that man arrays co-operate. Nations of slaves and divers have searched the sands of ocean and the bowels of earth for the pearls and diamonds which adorn the spectators. Transmitted as heirlooms from generation to generation, these treasures have shone on consecrated brows and could be the most faithful of historians had they speech. They know the joys and sorrows of the great and those of the small. Everywhere do they go; they are worn with pride at festivals, carried in despair to usurers, borne off in triumph amid blood and pillage, enshrined in masterpieces conceived by art for their protection. None, except the pearl of Cleopatra, has been lost. The Great and the Fortunate assemble to witness the coronation of some king, whose trappings are the work of men's hands, but the purple of whose raiment is less glorious than that of the flowers of the field. These festivals, splendid in light, bathed in music which the hand of man creates, aye, all the triumphs of that hand are subdued by a thought, crushed by a sentiment. The Mind can illumine in a man and round a man a light more vivid, can open his ear to more melodious harmonies, can seat him on clouds of shining constellations and teach him to question them. The Heart can do still greater things. Man may come into the presence of one sole being and find in a single word, a single look, an influence so weighty to bear, of so luminous a light, so penetrating a sound, that he succumbs and kneels before it. The most real of all splendors are not in outward things, they are within us. A single secret of science is a realm of wonders to the man of learning. Do the trumpets of Power, the jewels of Wealth, the music of Joy, or a vast concourse of people attend his mental festival? No, he finds his glory in some dim retreat where, perchance, a pallid suffering man whispers a single word into his ear; that word, like a torch lighted in a mine, reveals to him a Science. All human ideas, arrayed in every attractive form which Mystery can invent surrounded a blind man seated in a wayside ditch. Three worlds, the Natural, the Spiritual, the Divine, with all their spheres, opened their portals to a Florentine exile; he walked attended by the Happy and the Unhappy; by those who prayed and those who moaned; by angels and by souls in hell. When the Sent of God, who knew and could accomplish all things, appeared to three of his disciples it was at eventide, at the common table of the humblest of inns; and then and there the Light broke forth, shattering Material Forms, illuminating the Spiritual Faculties, so that they saw him in his glory, and the earth lay at their feet like a cast-off sandal.

Monsieur Becker, Wilfrid, and Minna were all under the influence of fear as they took their way to meet the extraordinary being whom each desired to question. To them, in their several ways, the Swedish castle had grown to mean some gigantic representation, some spectacle like those whose colors and masses are skilfully and harmoniously marshalled by the poets, and whose personages, imaginary actors to men, are real to those who begin to penetrate the Spiritual World. On the tiers of this Coliseum Monsieur Becker seated the gray legions of Doubt, the stern ideas, the specious formulas of Dispute. He convoked the various antagonistic worlds of philosophy and religion, and they all appeared, in the guise of a fleshless shape, like that in which art embodies Time,—an old man bearing in one hand a scythe, in the other a broken globe, the human universe.

Wilfrid had bidden to the scene his earliest illusions and his latest hopes, human destiny and its conflicts, religion and its conquering powers.

Minna saw heaven confusedly by glimpses; love raised a curtain wrought with mysterious images, and the melodious sounds which met her ear redoubled her curiosity.

To all three, therefore, this evening was to be what that other evening had been for the pilgrims to Emmaus, what a vision was to Dante, an inspiration to Homer,—to them, three aspects of the world revealed, veils rent away, doubts dissipated, darkness illumined. Humanity in all its moods expecting light could not be better represented than here by this young girl, this man in the vigor of his age, and these old men, of whom one was learned enough to doubt, the other ignorant enough to believe. Never was any scene more simple in appearance, nor more portentous in reality.

When they entered the room, ushered in by old David, they found Seraphita standing by a table on which were served the various dishes which compose a "tea"; a form of collation which in the North takes the place of wine and its pleasures,—reserved more exclusively for Southern climes. Certainly nothing proclaimed in her, or in him, a being with the strange power of appearing under two distinct forms; nothing about her betrayed the manifold powers which she wielded. Like a careful housewife attending to the comfort of her guests, she ordered David to put more wood into the stove.

"Good evening, my neighbors," she said. "Dear Monsieur Becker, you do right to come; you see me living for the last time, perhaps. This winter has killed me. Will you sit there?" she said to Wilfrid. "And you, Minna, here?" pointing to a chair beside her. "I see you have brought your embroidery. Did you invent that stitch? the design is very pretty. For whom is it,—your father, or monsieur?" she added, turning to Wilfrid. "Surely we ought to give him, before we part, a remembrance of the daughters of Norway."

"Did you suffer much yesterday?" asked Wilfrid.

"It was nothing," she answered; "the suffering gladdened me; it was necessary, to enable me to leave this life."

"Then death does not alarm you?" said Monsieur Becker, smiling, for he did not think her ill.

"No, dear pastor; there are two ways of dying: to some, death is victory, to others, defeat."

"Do you think that you have conquered?" asked Minna.

"I do not know," she said, "perhaps I have only taken a step in the path."

The lustrous splendor of her brow grew dim, her eyes were veiled beneath slow-dropping lids; a simple movement which affected the prying guests and kept them silent. Monsieur Becker was the first to recover courage.

"Dear child," he said, "you are truth itself, and you are ever kind. I would ask of you to-night something other than the dainties of your tea-table. If we may believe certain persons, you know amazing things; if this be true, would it not be charitable in you to solve a few of our doubts?"

"Ah!" she said smiling, "I walk on the clouds. I visit the depths of the fiord; the sea is my steed and I bridle it; I know where the singing flower grows, and the talking light descends, and fragrant colors shine! I wear the seal of Solomon; I am a fairy; I cast my orders to the wind which, like an abject slave, fulfils them; my eyes can pierce the earth and behold its treasures; for lo! am I not the virgin to whom the pearls dart from their ocean depths and—"

"—who led me safely to the summit of the Falberg?" said Minna, interrupting her.

"Thou! thou too!" exclaimed the strange being, with a luminous glance at the young girl which filled her soul with trouble. "Had I not the faculty of reading through your foreheads the desires which have brought you here, should I be what you think I am?" she said, encircling all three with her controlling glance, to David's great satisfaction. The old man rubbed his hands with pleasure as he left the room.

"Ah!" she resumed after a pause, "you have come, all of you, with the curiosity of children. You, my poor Monsieur Becker, have asked yourself how it was possible that a girl of seventeen should know even a single one of those secrets which men of science seek with their noses to the earth,—instead of raising their eyes to heaven. Were I to tell you how and at what point the plant merges into the animal you would begin to doubt your doubts. You have plotted to question me; you will admit that?"

"Yes, dear Seraphita," answered Wilfrid; "but the desire is a natural one to men, is it not?"

"You will bore this dear child with such topics," she said, passing her hand lightly over Minna's hair with a caressing gesture.

The young girl raised her eyes and seemed as though she longed to lose herself in him.

"Speech is the endowment of us all," resumed the mysterious creature, gravely. "Woe to him who keeps silence, even in a desert, believing that no one hears him; all voices speak and all ears listen here below. Speech moves the universe. Monsieur Becker, I desire to say nothing unnecessarily. I know the difficulties that beset your mind; would you not think it a miracle if I were now to lay bare the past history of your consciousness? Well, the miracle shall be accomplished. You have never admitted to yourself the full extent of your doubts. I alone, immovable in my faith, I can show it to you; I can terrify you with yourself.

"You stand on the darkest side of Doubt. You do not believe in God,—although you know it not,—and all things here below are secondary to him who rejects the first principle of things. Let us leave aside the fruitless discussions of false philosophy. The spiritualist generations made as many and as vain efforts to deny Matter as the materialist generations have made to deny Spirit. Why such discussions? Does not man himself offer irrefragable proof of both systems? Do we not find in him material things and spiritual things? None but a madman can refuse to see in the human body a fragment of Matter; your natural sciences, when they decompose it, find little difference between its elements and those of other animals. On the other hand, the idea produced in man by the comparison of many objects has never seemed to any one to belong to the domain of Matter. As to this, I offer no opinion. I am now concerned with your doubts, not with my certainties. To you, as to the majority of thinkers, the relations between things, the reality of which is proved to you by your sensations and which you possess the faculty to discover, do not seem Material. The Natural universe of things and beings ends, in man, with the Spiritual universe of similarities or differences which he perceives among the innumerable forms of Nature,—relations so multiplied as to seem infinite; for if, up to the present time, no one has been able to enumerate the separate terrestrial creations, who can reckon their correlations? Is not the fraction which you know, in relation to their totality, what a single number is to infinity? Here, then, you fall into a perception of the infinite which undoubtedly obliges you to conceive of a purely Spiritual world.

"Thus man himself offers sufficient proof of the two orders,— Matter and Spirit. In him culminates a visible finite universe; in him begins a universe invisible and infinite,—two worlds unknown to each other. Have the pebbles of the fiord a perception of their combined being? have they a consciousness of the colors they present to the eye of man? do they hear the music of the waves that lap them? Let us therefore spring over and not attempt to sound the abysmal depths presented to our minds in the union of a Material universe and a Spiritual universe,—a creation visible, ponderable, tangible, terminating in a creation invisible, imponderable, intangible; completely dissimilar, separated by the void, yet united by indisputable bonds and meeting in a being who derives equally from the one and from the other! Let us mingle in one world these two worlds, absolutely irreconcilable to your philosophies, but conjoined by fact. However abstract man may suppose the relation which binds two things together, the line of junction is perceptible. How? Where? We are not now in search of the vanishing point where Matter subtilizes. If such were the question, I cannot see why He who has, by physical relations, studded with stars at immeasurable distances the heavens which veil Him, may not have created solid substances, nor why you deny Him the faculty of giving a body to thought.

"Thus your invisible moral universe and your visible physical universe are one and the same matter. We will not separate properties from substances, nor objects from effects. All that exists, all that presses upon us and overwhelms us from above or from below, before us or in us, all that which our eyes and our minds perceive, all these named and unnamed things compose—in order to fit the problem of Creation to the measure of your logic—a block of finite Matter; but were it infinite, God would still not be its master. Now, reasoning with your views, dear pastor, no matter in what way God the infinite is concerned with this block of finite Matter, He cannot exist and retain the attributes with which man invests Him. Seek Him in facts, and He is not; spiritually and materially, you have made God impossible. Listen to the Word of human Reason forced to its ultimate conclusions.

"In bringing God face to face with the Great Whole, we see that only two states are possible between them,—either God and Matter are contemporaneous, or God existed alone before Matter. Were

Reason—the light that has guided the human race from the dawn of its existence—accumulated in one brain, even that mighty brain could not invent a third mode of being without suppressing both Matter and God. Let human philosophies pile mountain upon mountain of words and of ideas, let religions accumulate images and beliefs, revelations and mysteries, you must face at last this terrible dilemma and choose between the two propositions which compose it; you have no option, and one as much as the other leads human reason to Doubt.

"The problem thus established, what signifies Spirit or Matter? Why trouble about the march of the worlds in one direction or in another, since the Being who guides them is shown to be an absurdity? Why continue to ask whether man is approaching heaven or receding from it, whether creation is rising towards Spirit or descending towards Matter, if the questioned universe gives no reply? What signifies theogonies and their armies, theologies and their dogmas, since whichever side of the problem is man's choice, his God exists not? Let us for a moment take up the first proposition, and suppose God contemporaneous with Matter. Is subjection to the action or the co-existence of an alien substance consistent with being God at all? In such a system, would not God become a secondary agent compelled to organize Matter? If so, who compelled Him? Between His material gross companion and Himself, who was the arbiter? Who paid the wages of the six days' labor imputed to the great Designer? Has any determining force been found which was neither God nor Matter? God being regarded as the manufacturer of the machinery of the worlds, is it not as ridiculous to call Him God as to call the slave who turns the grindstone a Roman citizen? Besides, another difficulty, as insoluble to this supreme human reason as it is to God, presents itself.

"If we carry the problem higher, shall we not be like the Hindus, who put the world upon a tortoise, the tortoise on an elephant, and do not know on what the feet of their elephant may rest? This supreme will, issuing from the contest between God and Matter, this God, this more than God, can He have existed throughout eternity without willing what He afterwards willed,—

admitting that Eternity can be divided into two eras. No matter where God is, what becomes of His intuitive intelligence if He did not know His ultimate thought? Which, then, is the true Eternity,—the created Eternity or the uncreated? But if God throughout all time did will the world such as it is, this new necessity, which harmonizes with the idea of sovereign intelligence, implies the co-eternity of Matter. Whether Matter be co-eternal by a divine will necessarily accordant with itself from the beginning, or whether Matter be co-eternal of its own being, the power of God, which must be absolute, perishes if His will is circumscribed; for in that case God would find within Him a determining force which would control Him. Can He be God if He can no more separate Himself from His creation in a past eternity than in the coming eternity?

"This face of the problem is insoluble in its cause. Let us now inquire into its effects. If a God compelled to have created the world from all eternity seems inexplicable, He is quite as unintelligible in perpetual cohesion with His work. God, constrained to live eternally united to His creation is held down to His first position as workman. Can you conceive of a God who shall be neither independent of nor dependent on His work? Could He destroy that work without challenging Himself? Ask yourself, and decide! Whether He destroys it some day, or whether He never destroys it, either way is fatal to the attributes without which God cannot exist. Is the world an experiment? is it a perishable form to which destruction must come? If it is, is not God inconsistent and impotent? inconsistent, because He ought to have seen the result before the attempt,—moreover why should He delay to destroy that which He is to destroy?—impotent, for how else could He have created an imperfect man?

"If an imperfect creation contradicts the faculties which man attributes to God we are forced back upon the question, Is creation perfect? The idea is in harmony with that of a God supremely intelligent who could make no mistakes; but then, what means the degradation of His work, and its regeneration? Moreover, a perfect world is, necessarily, indestructible; its forms would not perish, it could neither advance nor recede, it would revolve in the everlasting circumference from which it would never issue. In that case God would be dependent on His work; it would be co-eternal with Him; and so we fall back into one of the propositions most antagonistic to God. If the world is imperfect, it can progress; if perfect, it is stationary. On the other hand, if it be impossible to admit of a progressive God ignorant through a past eternity of the results of His creative work, can there be a stationary God? would not that imply the triumph of Matter? would it not be the greatest of all negations? Under the first hypothesis God perishes through weakness; under the second through the Force of his inertia.

"Therefore, to all sincere minds the supposition that Matter, in the conception and execution of the worlds, is contemporaneous with God, is to deny God. Forced to choose, in order to govern the nations, between the two alternatives of the problem, whole generations have preferred this solution of it. Hence the doctrine of the two principles of Magianism, brought from Asia and adopted in Europe under the form of Satan warring with the Eternal Father. But this religious formula and the innumerable aspects of divinity that have sprung from it are surely crimes against the Majesty Divine. What other term can we apply to the belief which sets up as a rival to God a personification of Evil, striving eternally against the Omnipotent Mind without the possibility of ultimate triumph? Your statics declare that two Forces thus pitted against each other are reciprocally rendered null.

"Do you turn back, therefore, to the other side of the problem, and say that God pre-existed, original, alone?

"I will not go over the preceding arguments (which here return in full force) as to the severance of Eternity into two parts; nor the questions raised by the progression or the immobility of the worlds; let us look only at the difficulties inherent to this second theory. If God pre-existed alone, the world must have emanated from Him; Matter was therefore drawn from His essence; consequently Matter in itself is non-existent; all forms are veils to cover the Divine Spirit. If this be so, the World is Eternal, and also it must be God. Is not this proposition even more fatal than the former to the attributes conferred on God by human reason? How can the actual condition of Matter be explained if we suppose it to issue from the bosom of God and to be ever united with Him? Is it possible to believe that the All-Powerful, supremely good in His essence and in His faculties, has engendered things dissimilar to Himself. Must He not in all things and through all things be like unto Himself? Can there be in God certain evil parts of which at some future day he may rid Himself?—a conjecture less offensive and absurd than terrible, for the reason that it drags back into Him the two principles which the preceding theory proved to be inadmissible. God must be ONE; He cannot be divided without renouncing the most important condition of His existence. It is therefore impossible to admit of a fraction of God which yet is not God. This hypothesis seemed so criminal to the Roman Church that she has made the omnipresence of God in the least particles of the Eucharist an article of faith.

"But how then can we imagine an omnipotent mind which does not triumph? How associate it unless in triumph with Nature? But Nature is not triumphant; she seeks, combines, remodels, dies, and is born again; she is even more convulsed when creating than when all was fusion; Nature suffers, groans, is ignorant, degenerates, does evil; deceives herself, annihilates herself, disappears, and begins again. If God is associated with Nature, how can we explain the inoperative indifference of the divine principle? Wherefore death? How came it that Evil, king of the earth, was born of a God supremely good in His essence and in His faculties, who can produce nothing that is not made in His own image?

"But if, from this relentless conclusion which leads at once to absurdity, we pass to details, what end are we to assign to the world? If all is God, all is reciprocally cause and effect; all is One as God is One, and we can perceive neither points of likeness nor points of difference. Can the real end be a rotation of Matter which subtilizes and disappears? In whatever sense it were done, would not this mechanical trick of Matter issuing from God and returning to God seem a sort of child's play? Why should God make himself gross with Matter? Under which form is he most God? Which has the ascendant, Matter or Spirit, when neither can in any way do wrong? Who can comprehend the Deity engaged in this perpetual business, by which he divides Himself into two Natures, one of which knows nothing, while the other knows all? Can you conceive of God amusing Himself in the form of man, laughing at His own efforts, dying Friday, to be born again Sunday, and continuing this play from age to age, knowing the end from all eternity, and telling nothing to Himself, the Creature, of what He the Creator, does? The God of the preceding hypothesis, a God so nugatory by the very power of His inertia, seems the more possible of the two if we are compelled to choose between the impossibilities with which this God, so dull a jester, fusillades Himself when two sections of humanity argue face to face, weapons in hand.

"However absurd this outcome of the second problem may seem, it was adopted by half the human race in the sunny lands where smiling mythologies were created. Those amorous nations were consistent; with them all was God, even Fear and its dastardy, even crime and its bacchanals. If we accept pantheism,—the religion of many a great human genius,—who shall say where the greater reason lies? Is it with the savage, free in the desert, clothed in his nudity, listening to the sun, talking to the sea, sublime and always true in his deeds whatever they may be; or shall we find it in civilized man, who derives his chief enjoyments through lies; who wrings Nature and all her resources to put a musket on his shoulder; who employs his intellect to hasten the hour of his death and to create diseases out of pleasures? When the rake of pestilence and the ploughshare of war and the demon of desolation have passed over a corner of the globe and obliterated all things, who will be found to have the greater reason,—the Nubian savage or the patrician of Thebes? Your doubts descend the scale, they go from heights to depths, they embrace all, the end as well as the means.

"But if the physical world seems inexplicable, the moral world presents still stronger arguments against God. Where, then, is progress? If all things are indeed moving toward perfection why do we die young? why do not nations perpetuate themselves? The world having issued from God and being contained in God can it be stationary? Do we live once, or do we live always? If we live once, hurried onward by the march of the Great-Whole, a knowledge of which has not been given to us, let us act as we please. If we are eternal, let things take their course. Is the created being guilty if he exists at the instant of the transitions? If he sins at the moment of a great transformation will he be punished for it after being its victim? What becomes of the Divine goodness if we are not transferred to the regions of the blest—should any such exist? What becomes of God's prescience if He is ignorant of the results of the trials to which He subjects us? What is this alternative offered to man by all religions,—either to boil in some eternal cauldron or to walk in white robes, a palm in his hand and a halo round his head? Can it be that this pagan invention is the final word of God? Where is the generous soul who does not feel that the calculating virtue which seeks the eternity of pleasure offered by all religions to whoever fulfils at stray moments certain fanciful and often unnatural conditions, is unworthy of man and of God? Is it not a mockery to give to man impetuous senses and forbid him to satisfy them? Besides, what mean these ascetic objections if Good and Evil are equally abolished? Does Evil exist? If substance in all its forms is God, then Evil is God. The faculty of reasoning as well as the faculty of feeling having been given to man to use, nothing can be more excusable in him than to seek to know the meaning of human suffering and the prospects of the future.

"If these rigid and rigorous arguments lead to such conclusions confusion must reign. The world would have no fixedness; nothing would advance, nothing would pause, all would change, nothing would be destroyed, all would reappear after self-renovation; for if your mind does not clearly demonstrate to you an end, it is equally impossible to demonstrate the destruction of the smallest particle of Matter; Matter can transform but not annihilate itself.

"Though blind force may provide arguments for the atheist, intelligent force is inexplicable; for if it emanates from God, why should it meet with obstacles? ought not its triumph to be immediate? Where is God? If the living cannot perceive Him, can the dead find Him? Crumble, ye idolatries and ye religions! Fall, feeble keystones of all social arches, powerless to retard the decay, the death, the oblivion that have overtaken all nations however firmly founded! Fall, morality and justice! our crimes are purely relative; they are divine effects whose causes we are not allowed to know. All is God. Either we are God or God is not!—Child of a century whose every year has laid upon your brow, old man, the ice of its unbelief, here, here is the summing up of your lifetime of

88

thought, of your science and your reflections! Dear Monsieur Becker, you have laid your head upon the pillow of Doubt, because it is the easiest of solutions; acting in this respect with the majority of mankind, who say in their hearts: 'Let us think no more of these problems, since God has not vouchsafed to grant us the algebraic demonstrations that could solve them, while He has given us so many other ways to get from earth to heaven.'

"Tell me, dear pastor, are not these your secret thoughts? Have I evaded the point of any? nay, rather, have I not clearly stated all? First, in the dogma of two principles,—an antagonism in which God perishes for the reason that being All-Powerful He chose to combat. Secondly, in the absurd pantheism where, all being God, God exists no longer. These two sources, from which have flowed all the religions for whose triumph Earth has toiled and prayed, are equally pernicious. Behold in them the double-bladed axe with which you decapitate the white old man whom you enthrone among your painted clouds! And now, to me the axe, I wield it!"

Monsieur Becker and Wilfrid gazed at the young girl with something like terror.

"To believe," continued Seraphita, in her Woman's voice, for the Man had finished speaking, "to believe is a gift. To believe is to feel. To believe in God we must feel God. This feeling is a possession slowly acquired by the human being, just as other astonishing powers which you admire in great men, warriors, artists, scholars, those who know and those who act, are acquired. Thought, that budget of the relations which you perceive among created things, is an intellectual language which can be learned, is it not? Belief, the budget of celestial truths, is also a language as superior to thought as thought is to instinct. This language also can be learned. The Believer answers with a single cry, a single gesture; Faith puts within his hand a flaming sword with which he pierces and illumines all. The Seer attains to heaven and descends not. But there are beings who believe and see, who know and will, who love and pray and wait. Submissive, yet aspiring to the kingdom of light, they have neither the aloofness of the Believer nor the silence of the Seer; they listen and reply. To them the doubt of the twilight ages is not a murderous weapon, but a divining rod; they accept the contest under every form; they train their tongues to every language; they are never angered, though they groan; the acrimony of the aggressor is not in them, but rather the softness and tenuity of light, which penetrates and warms and illumines. To their eyes Doubt is neither an impiety, nor a blasphemy, nor a crime, but a transition through which men return upon their steps in the Darkness, or advance into the Light. This being so, dear pastor, let us reason together.

"You do not believe in God? Why? God, to your thinking, is incomprehensible, inexplicable. Agreed. I will not reply that to comprehend God in His entirety would be to be God; nor will I tell you that you deny what seems to you inexplicable so as to give me the right to affirm that which to me is believable. There is, for you, one evident fact, which lies within yourself. In you, Matter has ended in intelligence; can you therefore think that human intelligence will end in darkness, doubt, and nothingness? God may seem to you incomprehensible and inexplicable, but you must admit Him to be, in all things purely physical, a splendid and consistent workman. Why should His craft stop short at man, His most finished creation?

"If that question is not convincing, at least it compels meditation. Happily, although you deny God, you are obliged, in order to establish your doubts, to admit those double-bladed facts, which kill your arguments as much as your arguments kill God. We have also admitted that Matter and Spirit are two creations which do not comprehend each other; that the spiritual world is formed of infinite relations to which the finite material world has given rise; that if no one on earth is able to identify himself by the power of his spirit with the great-whole of terrestrial creations, still less is he able to rise to the knowledge of the relations which the spirit perceives between these creations.

"We might end the argument here in one word, by denying you the faculty of comprehending God, just as you deny to the pebbles of the fiord the faculties of counting and of seeing each other. How do you know that the stones themselves do not deny the existence of man, though man makes use of them to build his houses? There is one fact that appals you,—the Infinite; if you feel it within, why will you not admit its consequences? Can the finite have a perfect knowledge of the infinite? If you cannot perceive those relations which, according to your own admission, are infinite, how can you grasp a sense of the far-off end to which they are converging? Order, the revelation of which is one of your needs, being infinite, can your limited reason apprehend it? Do not ask why man does not comprehend that which he is able to perceive, for he is equally able to perceive that which he does not comprehend. If I prove to you that your mind ignores that which lies within its compass, will you grant that it is impossible for it to conceive whatever is beyond it? This being so, am I not justified in saying to you: 'One of the two propositions under which God is annihilated before the tribunal of our reason must be true, the other is false. Inasmuch as creation exists, you feel the necessity of an end, and that end should be good, should it not? Now, if Matter terminates in man by intelligence, why are you not satisfied to believe that the end of human intelligence is the Light of the higher spheres, where alone an intuition of that God who seems so insoluble a problem is obtained? The species which are beneath you have no conception of the universe, and you have; why should there not be other species above you more intelligent than your own? Man ought to be better informed than he is about himself before he spends his strength in measuring God. Before attacking the stars that light us, and the higher certainties, ought he not to understand the certainties which are actually about him?'

"But no! to the negations of doubt I ought rather to reply by negations. Therefore I ask you whether there is anything here below so evident that I can put faith in it? I will show you in a moment that you believe firmly in things which act, and yet are not beings; in things which engender thought, and yet are not spirits; in living abstractions which the understanding cannot grasp in any shape, which are in fact nowhere, but which you perceive everywhere; which have, and can have, on name, but which, nevertheless, you have named; and which, like the God of flesh upon whom you figure to yourself, remain inexplicable, incomprehensible, and absurd. I shall also ask you why, after

91

admitting the existence of these incomprehensible things, you reserve your doubts for God?

"You believe, for instance, in Number,—a base on which you have built the edifice of sciences which you call 'exact.' Without Number, what would become of mathematics? Well, what mysterious being endowed with the faculty of living forever could utter, and what language would be compact to word the Number which contains the infinite numbers whose existence is revealed to you by thought? Ask it of the loftiest human genius; he might ponder it for a thousand years and what would be his answer? You know neither where Number begins, nor where it pauses, nor where it ends. Here you call it Time, there you call it Space. Nothing exists except by Number. Without it, all would be one and the same substance; for Number alone differentiates and qualifies substance. Number is to your Spirit what it is to Matter, an incomprehensible agent. Will you make a Deity of it? Is it a being? Is it a breath emanating from God to organize the material universe where nothing obtains form except by the Divinity which is an effect of Number? The least as well as the greatest of creations are distinguishable from each other by quantities, qualities, dimensions, forces,—all attributes created by Number. The infinitude of Numbers is a fact proved to your soul, but of which no material proof can be given. The mathematician himself tells you that the infinite of numbers exists, but cannot be proved.

"God, dear pastor, is a Number endowed with motion,—felt, but not seen, the Believer will tell you. Like the Unit, He begins Number, with which He has nothing in common. The existence of Number depends on the Unit, which without being a number engenders Number. God, dear pastor is a glorious Unit who has nothing in common with His creations but who, nevertheless, engenders them. Will you not therefore agree with me that you are just as ignorant of where Number begins and ends as you are of where created Eternity begins and ends?

"Why, then, if you believe in Number, do you deny God? Is not Creation interposed between the Infinite of unorganized substances and the Infinite of the divine spheres, just as the Unit stands between the Cipher of the fractions you have lately named Decimals, and the Infinite of Numbers which you call Wholes? Man alone on earth comprehends Number, that first step of the peristyle which leads to God, and yet his reason stumbles on it! What! you can neither measure nor grasp the first abstraction which God delivers to you, and yet you try to subject His ends to your own tape-line! Suppose that I plunge you into the abyss of Motion, the force that organizes Number. If I tell you that the Universe is naught else than Number and Motion, you would see at once that we speak two different languages. I understand them both; you understand neither.

"Suppose I add that Motion and Number are engendered by the Word, namely the supreme Reason of Seers and Prophets who in the olden time heard the Breath of God beneath which Saul fell to the earth. That Word, you scoff at it, you men, although you well know that all visible works, societies, monuments, deeds, passions, proceed from the breath of your own feeble word, and that without that word you would resemble the African gorilla, the nearest approach to man, the Negro. You believe firmly in Number and in Motion, a force and a result both inexplicable, incomprehensible, to the existence of which I may apply the logical dilemma which, as we have seen, prevents you from believing in God. Powerful reasoner that you are, you do not need that I should prove to you that the Infinite must everywhere be like unto Itself, and that, necessarily, it is One. God alone is Infinite, for surely there cannot be two Infinities, two Ones. If, to make use of human terms, anything demonstrated to you here below seems to you infinite, be sure that within it you will find some one aspect of God. But to continue.

"You have appropriated to yourself a place in the Infinite of Number; you have fitted it to your own proportions by creating (if indeed you did create) arithmetic, the basis on which all things rest, even your societies. Just as Number—the only thing in which your self-styled atheists believe—organized physical creations, so arithmetic, in the employ of Number, organized the moral world. This numeration must be absolute, like all else that is true in itself;

but it is purely relative, it does not exist absolutely, and no proof can be given of its reality. In the first place, though Numeration is able to take account of organized substances, it is powerless in relation to unorganized forces, the ones being finite and the others infinite. The man who can conceive the Infinite by his intelligence cannot deal with it in its entirety; if he could, he would be God. Your Numeration, applying to things finite and not to the Infinite, is therefore true in relation to the details which you are able to perceive, and false in relation to the Whole, which you are unable to perceive. Though Nature is like unto herself in the organizing force or in her principles which are infinite, she is not so in her finite effects. Thus you will never find in Nature two objects identically alike. In the Natural Order two and two never make four; to do so, four exactly similar units must be had, and you know how impossible it is to find two leaves alike on the same tree, or two trees alike of the same species. This axiom of your numeration, false in visible nature, is equally false in the invisible universe of your abstractions, where the same variance takes place in your ideas, which are the things of the visible world extended by means of their relations; so that the variations here are even more marked than elsewhere. In fact, all being relative to the temperament, strength, habits, and customs of individuals, who never resemble each other, the smallest objects take the color of personal feelings. For instance, man has been able to create units and to give an equal weight and value to bits of gold. Well, take the ducat of the rich man and the ducat of the poor man to a money-changer and they are rated exactly equal, but to the mind of the thinker one is of greater importance than the other; one represents a month of comfort, the other an ephemeral caprice. Two and two, therefore, only make four through a false conception.

"Again: fraction does not exist in Nature, where what you call a fragment is a finished whole. Does it not often happen (have you not many proofs of it?) that the hundredth part of a substance is stronger than what you term the whole of it? If fraction does not exist in the Natural Order, still less shall we find it in the Moral Order, where ideas and sentiments may be as varied as the species of the Vegetable kingdom and yet be always whole. The theory of fractions is therefore another signal instance of the servility of your mind.

"Thus Number, with its infinite minuteness and its infinite expansion, is a power whose weakest side is known to you, but whose real import escapes your perception. You have built yourself a hut in the Infinite of numbers, you have adorned it with hieroglyphics scientifically arranged and painted, and you cry out, 'All is here!'

"Let us pass from pure, unmingled Number to corporate Number. Your geometry establishes that a straight line is the shortest way from one point to another, but your astronomy proves that God has proceeded by curves. Here, then, we find two truths equally proved by the same science, — one by the testimony of your senses reinforced by the telescope, the other by the testimony of your mind; and yet the one contradicts the other. Man, liable to err, affirms one, and the Maker of the worlds, whom, so far, you have not detected in error, contradicts it. Who shall decide between rectalinear and curvilinear geometry? between the theory of the straight line and that of the curve? If, in His vast work, the mysterious Artificer, who knows how to reach His ends miraculously fast, never employs a straight line except to cut off an angle and so obtain a curve, neither does man himself always rely upon it. The bullet which he aims direct proceeds by a curve, and when you wish to strike a certain point in space, you impel your bombshell along its cruel parabola. None of your men of science have drawn from this fact the simple deduction that the Curve is the law of the material worlds and the Straight line that of the Spiritual worlds; one is the theory of finite creations, the other the theory of the infinite. Man, who alone in the world has a knowledge of the Infinite, can alone know the straight line; he alone has the sense of verticality placed in a special organ. A fondness for the creations of the curve would seem to be in certain men an indication of the impurity of their nature still conjoined to the material substances which engender us; and the love of great souls for the straight line seems to show in them an intuition of heaven. Between these two lines there is a gulf fixed like that between the finite and the infinite, between matter and spirit, between man and the idea, between motion and the object moved, between the creature and God. Ask Love the Divine to grant you his wings and you can cross that gulf. Beyond it begins the revelation of the Word.

"No part of those things which you call material is without its own meaning; lines are the boundaries of solid parts and imply a force of action which you suppress in your formulas,—thus rendering those formulas false in relation to substances taken as a whole. Hence the constant destruction of the monuments of human labor, which you supply, unknown to yourselves, with acting properties. Nature has substances; your science combines only their appearances. At every step Nature gives the lie to all your laws. Can you find a single one that is not disproved by a fact? Your Static laws are at the mercy of a thousand accidents; a fluid can overthrow a solid mountain and prove that the heaviest substances may be lifted by one that is imponderable.

"Your laws on Acoustics and Optics are defied by the sounds which you hear within yourselves in sleep, and by the light of an electric sun whose rays often overcome you. You know no more how light makes itself seen within you, than you know the simple and natural process which changes it on the throats of tropic birds to rubies, sapphires, emeralds, and opals, or keeps it gray and brown on the breasts of the same birds under the cloudy skies of Europe, or whitens it here in the bosom of our polar Nature. You know not how to decide whether color is a faculty with which all substances are endowed, or an effect produced by an effluence of light. You admit the saltness of the sea without being able to prove that the water is salt at its greatest depth. You recognize the existence of various substances which span what you think to be the void,—substances which are not tangible under any of the forms assumed by Matter, although they put themselves in harmony with Matter in spite of every obstacle.

"All this being so, you believe in the results of Chemistry, although that science still knows no way of gauging the changes produced by the flux and reflux of substances which come and go across your crystals and your instruments on the impalpable filaments of heat or light conducted and projected by the affinities of metal or vitrified flint. You obtain none but dead substances, from which you have driven the unknown force that holds in check the decomposition of all things here below, and of which cohesion, attraction, vibration, and polarity are but phenomena. Life is the thought of substances; bodies are only the means of fixing life and holding it to its way. If bodies were beings living of themselves they would be Cause itself, and could not die.

"When a man discovers the results of the general movement, which is shared by all creations according to their faculty of absorption, you proclaim him mighty in science, as though genius consisted in explaining a thing that is! Genius ought to cast its eyes beyond effects. Your men of science would laugh if you said to them: 'There exist such positive relations between two human beings, one of whom may be here, and the other in Java, that they can at the same instant feel the same sensation, and be conscious of so doing; they can question each other and reply without mistake'; and yet there are mineral substances which exhibit sympathies as far off from each other as those of which I speak. You believe in the power of the electricity which you find in the magnet and you deny that which emanates from the soul! According to you, the moon, whose influence upon the tides you think fixed, has none whatever upon the winds, nor upon navigation, nor upon men; she moves the sea, but she must not affect the sick folk; she has undeniable relations with one half of humanity, and nothing at all to do with the other half. These are your vaunted certainties!

"Let us go a step further. You believe in physics. But your physics begin, like the Catholic religion, with an act of faith. Do they not pre-suppose some external force distinct from substance to which it communicates motion? You see its effects, but what is it? where is it? what is the essence of its nature, its life? has it any limits?—and yet, you deny God!

"Thus, the majority of your scientific axioms, true to their relation to man, are false in relation to the Great Whole. Science is One, but you have divided it. To know the real meaning of the laws of phenomena must we not know the correlations which exist between phenomena and the law of the Whole? There is, in all things, an appearance which strikes your senses; under that appearance stirs a soul; a body is there and a faculty is there. Where do you teach the study of the relations which bind things to each other? Nowhere. Consequently you have nothing positive. Your strongest certainties rest upon the analysis of material forms whose essence you persistently ignore.

"There is a Higher Knowledge of which, too late, some men obtain a glimpse, though they dare not avow it. Such men comprehend the necessity of considering substances not merely in their mathematical properties but also in their entirety, in their occult relations and affinities. The greatest man among you divined, in his latter days, that all was reciprocally cause and effect; that the visible worlds were co-ordinated among themselves and subject to worlds invisible. He groaned at the recollection of having tried to establish fixed precepts. Counting up his worlds, like grape-seeds scattered through ether, he had explained their coherence by the laws of planetary and molecular attraction. You bowed before that man of science—well! I tell you that he died in despair. By supposing that the centrifugal and centripetal forces, which he had invented to explain to himself the universe, were equal, he stopped the universe; yet he admitted motion in an indeterminate sense; but supposing those forces unequal, then utter confusion of the planetary system ensued. His laws therefore were not absolute; some higher problem existed than the principle on which his false glory rested. The connection of the stars with one another and the centripetal action of their internal motion did not deter him from seeking the parent stalk on which his clusters hung. Alas, poor man! the more he widened space the heavier his burden grew. He told you how there came to be equilibrium among the parts, but whither went the whole? His mind contemplated the vast extent, illimitable to human eyes, filled with those groups of worlds a mere fraction of which is all our telescopes can reach, but whose immensity is revealed by the rapidity of light. This sublime contemplation enabled him to perceive myriads of worlds, planted in space like flowers in a field, which are born like infants, grow like men, die as the aged die, and live by assimilating from their atmosphere the substances suitable for their nourishment,—having a centre and a principal of life, guaranteeing to each other their circuits, absorbed and absorbing like plants, and forming a vast Whole endowed with life and possessing a destiny.

"At that sight your man of science trembled! He knew that life is produced by the union of the thing and its principle, that death or inertia or gravity is produced by a rupture between a thing and the movement which appertains to it. Then it was that he foresaw the crumbling of the worlds and their destruction if God should withdraw the Breath of His Word. He searched the Apocalypse for the traces of that Word. You thought him mad. Understand him better! He was seeking pardon for the work of his genius.

"Wilfrid, you have come here hoping to make me solve equations, or rise upon a rain-cloud, or plunge into the fiord and reappear a swan. If science or miracles were the end and object of humanity, Moses would have bequeathed to you the law of fluxions; Jesus Christ would have lightened the darkness of your sciences; his apostles would have told you whence come those vast trains of gas and melted metals, attached to cores which revolve and solidify as they dart through ether, or violently enter some system and combine with a star, jostling and displacing it by the shock, or destroying it by the infiltration of their deadly gases; Saint Paul, instead of telling you to live in God, would have explained why food is the secret bond among all creations and the evident tie between all living Species. In these days the greatest miracle of all would be the discovery of the squaring of the circle,—a problem which you hold to be insoluble, but which is doubtless solved in the march of worlds by the intersection of some mathematical lines whose course is visible to the eye of spirits who have reached the higher spheres. Believe me, miracles are in us, not without us. Here natural facts occur which men call supernatural. God would have been strangely unjust had he confined the testimony of his power to certain generations and peoples and denied them to others. The brazen rod belongs to all. Neither Moses, nor Jacob, nor Zoroaster, nor Paul, nor Pythagoras, nor Swedenborg, not the humblest Messenger nor the loftiest Prophet of the Most High are greater than you are capable of being. Only, there come to nations as to men certain periods when Faith is theirs.

"If material sciences be the end and object of human effort, tell me, both of you, would societies,—those great centres where men congregate,—would they perpetually be dispersed? If civilization were the object of our Species, would intelligence perish? would it continue purely individual? The grandeur of all nations that were truly great was based on exceptions; when the exception ceased their power died. If such were the End-all, Prophets, Seers, and Messengers of God would have lent their hand to Science rather than have given it to Belief. Surely they would have quickened your brains sooner than have touched your hearts! But no; one and all they came to lead the nations back to God; they proclaimed the sacred Path in simple words that showed the way to heaven; all were wrapped in love and faith, all were inspired by that word which hovers above the inhabitants of earth, enfolding them, inspiriting them, uplifting them; none were prompted by any human interest. Your great geniuses, your poets, your kings, your learned men are engulfed with their cities; while the names of these good pastors of humanity, ever blessed, have survived all cataclysms.

"Alas! we cannot understand each other on any point. We are separated by an abyss. You are on the side of darkness, while I—I live in the light, the true Light! Is this the word that you ask of me? I say it with joy; it may change you. Know this: there are sciences of matter and sciences of spirit. There, where you see substances, I see forces that stretch one toward another with generating power. To me, the character of bodies is the indication of their principles and the sign of their properties. Those principles beget affinities which escape your knowledge, and which are linked to centres. The different species among which life is distributed are unfailing streams which correspond unfailingly among themselves. Each has his own vocation. Man is effect and cause. He is fed, but he feeds in turn. When you call God a Creator, you dwarf Him. He did not create, as you think He did, plants or animals or stars. Could He proceed by a variety of means? Must He not act by unity of composition? Moreover, He gave forth principles to be developed, according to His universal law, at the will of the surroundings in which they were placed. Hence a single substance and motion, a single plant, a single animal, but correlations everywhere. In fact, all affinities are linked together by contiguous similitudes; the life of the worlds is drawn toward the centres by famished aspiration, as you are drawn by hunger to seek food.

"To give you an example of affinities linked to similitudes (a secondary law on which the creations of your thought are based), music, that celestial art, is the working out of this principle; for is it not a complement of sounds harmonized by number? Is not sound a modification of air, compressed, dilated, echoed? You know the composition of air,—oxygen, nitrogen, and carbon. As you cannot obtain sound from the void, it is plain that music and the human voice are the result of organized chemical substances, which put themselves in unison with the same substances prepared within you by your thought, co-ordinated by means of light, the great nourisher of your globe. Have you ever meditated on the masses of nitre deposited by the snow, have you ever observed a thunderstorm and seen the plants breathing in from the air about them the metal it contains, without concluding that the sun has fused and distributed the subtle essence which nourishes all things here below? Swedenborg has said, 'The earth is a man.'

"Your Science, which makes you great in your own eyes, is paltry indeed beside the light which bathes a Seer. Cease, cease to question me; our languages are different. For a moment I have used yours to cast, if it be possible, a ray of faith into your soul; to give you, as it were, the hem of my garment and draw you up into the regions of Prayer. Can God abase Himself to you? Is it not for you to rise to Him? If human reason finds the ladder of its own strength too weak to bring God down to it, is it not evident that you must find some other path to reach Him? That Path is in ourselves. The Seer and the Believer find eyes within their souls more piercing far than eyes that probe the things of earth,—they see the Dawn. Hear this truth: Your science, let it be never so exact, your meditations, however bold, your noblest lights are Clouds. Above, above is the Sanctuary whence the true Light flows."

She sat down and remained silent; her calm face bore no sign of the agitation which orators betray after their least fervid improvisations.

Wilfrid bent toward Monsieur Becker and said in a low voice, "Who taught her that?"

"I do not know," he answered.

"He was gentler on the Falberg," Minna whispered to herself.

Seraphita passed her hand across her eyes and then she said, smiling:—

"You are very thoughtful to-night, gentlemen. You treat Minna and me as though we were men to whom you must talk politics or commerce; whereas we are young girls, and you ought to tell us tales while you drink your tea. That is what we do, Monsieur Wilfrid, in our long Norwegian evenings. Come, dear pastor, tell me some Saga that I have not heard,—that of Frithiof, the chronicle that you believe and have so often promised me. Tell us the story of the peasant lad who owned the ship that talked and had a soul. Come! I dream of the frigate Ellida, the fairy with the sails young girls should navigate!"

"Since we have returned to the regions of Jarvis," said Wilfrid, whose eyes were fastened on Seraphita as those of a robber, lurking in the darkness, fasten on the spot where he knows the jewels lie, "tell me why you do not marry?"

"You are all born widows and widowers," she replied; "but my marriage was arranged at my birth. I am betrothed."

"To whom?" they cried.

"Ask not my secret," she said; "I will promise, if our father permits it, to invite you to these mysterious nuptials."

"Will they be soon?"

"I think so."

A long silence followed these words.

"The spring has come!" said Seraphita, suddenly. "The noise of the waters and the breaking of the ice begins. Come, let us welcome the first spring of the new century."

She rose, followed by Wilfrid, and together they went to a window which David had opened. After the long silence of winter, the waters stirred beneath the ice and resounded through the fiord like music,—for there are sounds which space refines, so that they reach the ear in waves of light and freshness.

"Wilfrid, cease to nourish evil thoughts whose triumph would be hard to bear. Your desires are easily read in the fire of your eyes. Be kind; take one step forward in well-doing. Advance beyond the love of man and sacrifice yourself completely to the happiness of her you love. Obey me; I will lead you in a path where you shall obtain the distinctions which you crave, and where Love is infinite indeed."

She left him thoughtful.

"That soft creature!" he said within himself; "is she indeed the prophetess whose eyes have just flashed lightnings, whose voice has rung through worlds, whose hand has wielded the axe of doubt against our sciences? Have we been dreaming? Am I awake?"

"Minna," said Seraphita, returning to the young girl, "the eagle swoops where the carrion lies, but the dove seeks the mountain spring beneath the peaceful greenery of the glades. The eagle soars to heaven, the dove descends from it. Cease to venture into regions where thou canst find no spring of waters, no umbrageous shade. If on the Falberg thou couldst not gaze into the abyss and live, keep all thy strength for him who will love thee. Go, poor girl; thou knowest, I am betrothed."

Minna rose and followed Seraphita to the window where Wilfrid stood. All three listened to the Sieg bounding out the rush of the upper waters, which brought down trees uprooted by the ice; the fiord had regained its voice; all illusions were dispelled! They rejoiced in Nature as she burst her bonds and seemed to answer with sublime accord to the Spirit whose breath had wakened her.

When the three guests of this mysterious being left the house, they were filled with the vague sensation which is neither sleep, nor torpor, nor astonishment, but partakes of the nature of each,—a state that is neither dusk nor dawn, but which creates a thirst for light. All three were thinking.

"I begin to believe that she is indeed a Spirit hidden in human form," said Monsieur Becker.

Wilfrid, re-entering his own apartments, calm and convinced, was unable to struggle against that influence so divinely majestic.

Minna said in her heart, "Why will he not let me love him!"

CHAPTER V

FAREWELL

There is in man an almost hopeless phenomenon for thoughtful minds who seek a meaning in the march of civilization, and who endeavor to give laws of progression to the movement of intelligence. However portentous a fact may be, or even supernatural,—if such facts exist,—however solemnly a miracle may be done in sight of all, the lightning of that fact, the thunderbolt of that miracle is quickly swallowed up in the ocean of life, whose surface, scarcely stirred by the brief convulsion, returns to the level of its habitual flow.

A Voice is heard from the jaws of an Animal; a Hand writes on the wall before a feasting Court; an Eye gleams in the slumber of a king, and a Prophet explains the dream; Death, evoked, rises on the confines of the luminous sphere were faculties revive; Spirit annihilates Matter at the foot of that mystic ladder of the Seven Spiritual Worlds, one resting upon another in space and revealing themselves in shining waves that break in light upon the steps of the celestial Tabernacle. But however solemn the inward Revelation, however clear the visible outward Sign, be sure that on the morrow Balaam doubts both himself and his ass, Belshazzar and Pharoah call Moses and Daniel to qualify the Word. The Spirit, descending, bears man above this earth, opens the seas and lets him see their depths, shows him lost species, wakens dry bones whose dust is the soil of valleys; the Apostle writes the Apocalypse, and twenty centuries later human science ratifies his words and turns his visions into maxims. And what comes of it all? Why this,—that the peoples live as they have ever lived, as they lived in the first Olympiad, as they lived on the morrow of Creation, and on the eve of the great cataclysm. The waves of Doubt have covered all things. The same floods surge with the same measured motion on the human granite which serves as a boundary to the ocean of intelligence. When man has inquired of himself whether he has seen that which he has seen, whether he has heard the words that entered his ears, whether the facts were facts and the idea is indeed an idea, then he resumes his wonted bearing, thinks of his worldly interests, obeys some envoy of death and of oblivion whose dusky mantle covers like a pall an ancient Humanity of which the moderns retain no memory. Man never pauses; he goes his round, he vegetates until the appointed day when his Axe falls. If this wave force, this pressure of bitter waters prevents all progress, no doubt it also warns of death. Spirits prepared by faith among the higher souls of earth can alone perceive the mystic ladder of Jacob.

After listening to Seraphita's answer in which (being earnestly questioned) she unrolled before their eyes a Divine Perspective,—as an organ fills a church with sonorous sound and reveals a musical universe, its solemn tones rising to the loftiest arches and playing, like light, upon their foliated capitals,—Wilfrid returned to his own room, awed by the sight of a world in ruins, and on those ruins the brilliance of mysterious lights poured forth in torrents by the hand of a young girl. On the morrow he still thought of these things, but his awe was gone; he felt he was neither destroyed nor changed; his passions, his ideas awoke in full force, fresh and vigorous. He went to breakfast with Monsieur Becker and found the old man absorbed in the "Treatise on Incantations," which he had searched since early morning to convince his guest that there was nothing unprecedented in all that they had seen and heard at the Swedish castle. With the childlike trustfulness of a true scholar he had folded down the pages in which Jean Wier related authentic facts which proved the possibility of the events that had happened the night before,—for to learned men an idea is a event, just as the greatest events often present no idea at all to them. By the time they had swallowed their fifth cup of tea, these philosophers had come to think the mysterious scene of the preceding evening wholly natural. The celestial truths to which they had listened were arguments susceptible of examination; Seraphita was a girl, more or less eloquent; allowance must be made for the charms of her voice, her seductive beauty, her fascinating motions, in short, for all those oratorical arts by which an actor puts a world of sentiment and thought into phrases which are often commonplace.

"Bah!" said the worthy pastor, making a philosophical grimace as he spread a layer of salt butter on his slice of bread, "the final word of all these fine enigmas is six feet under ground."

"But," said Wilfrid, sugaring his tea, "I cannot image how a young girl of seventeen can know so much; what she said was certainly a compact argument."

"Read the account of that Italian woman," said Monsieur Becker, "who at the age of twelve spoke forty-two languages, ancient and modern; also the history of that monk who could guess thought by smell. I can give you a thousand such cases from Jean Wier and other writers."

"I admit all that, dear pastor; but to my thinking, Seraphita would make a perfect wife."

"She is all mind," said Monsieur Becker, dubiously.

Several days went by, during which the snow in the valleys melted gradually away; the green of the forests and of the grass began to show; Norwegian Nature made ready her wedding garments for her brief bridal of a day. During this period, when the softened air invited every one to leave the house, Seraphita remained at home in solitude. When at last she admitted Minna the latter saw at once the ravages of inward fever; Seraphita's voice was hollow, her skin pallid; hitherto a poet might have compared her lustre to that of diamonds,—now it was that of a topaz.

"Have you seen her?" asked Wilfrid, who had wandered around the Swedish dwelling waiting for Minna's return.

"Yes," answered the young girl, weeping; "We must lose him!"

"Mademoiselle," cried Wilfrid, endeavoring to repress the loud tones of his angry voice, "do not jest with me. You can love Seraphita only as one young girl can love another, and not with the love which she inspires in me. You do not know your danger if my jealousy were really aroused. Why can I not go to her? Is it you who stand in my way?"

"I do not know by what right you probe my heart," said Minna, calm in appearance, but inwardly terrified. "Yes, I love him," she said, recovering the courage of her convictions, that she might, for once, confess the religion of her heart. "But my jealousy, natural as it is in love, fears no one here below. Alas! I am jealous of a secret feeling that absorbs him. Between him and me there is a great gulf fixed which I cannot cross. Would that I knew who loves him best, the stars or I! which of us would sacrifice our being most eagerly for his happiness! Why should I not be free to avow my love? In the presence of death we may declare our feelings,—and Seraphitus is about to die."

"Minna, you are mistaken; the siren I so love and long for, she, whom I have seen, feeble and languid, on her couch of furs, is not a young man."

"Monsieur," answered Minna, distressfully, "the being whose powerful hand guided me on the Falberg, who led me to the saeter sheltered beneath the Ice-Cap, there—" she said, pointing to the peak, "is not a feeble girl. Ah, had you but heard him prophesying! His poem was the music of thought. A young girl never uttered those solemn tones of a voice which stirred my soul."

"What certainty have you?" said Wilfrid.

"None but that of the heart," answered Minna.

"And I," cried Wilfrid, casting on his companion the terrible glance of the earthly desire that kills, "I, too, know how powerful is her empire over me, and I will undeceive you."

At this moment, while the words were rushing from Wilfrid's lips as rapidly as the thoughts surged in his brain, they saw Seraphita coming towards them from the house, followed by David. The apparition calmed the man's excitement.

"Look," he said, "could any but a woman move with that grace and langor?"

"He suffers; he comes forth for the last time," said Minna.

David went back at a sign from his mistress, who advanced towards Wilfrid and Minna.

"Let us go to the falls of the Sieg," she said, expressing one of those desires which suddenly possess the sick and which the well hasten to obey.

A thin white mist covered the valleys around the fiord and the sides of the mountains, whose icy summits, sparkling like stars, pierced the vapor and gave it the appearance of a moving milky way. The sun was visible through the haze like a globe of red fire. Though winter still lingered, puffs of warm air laden with the scent of the birch-trees, already adorned with their rosy efflorescence, and of the larches, whose silken tassels were beginning to appear,— breezes tempered by the incense and the sighs of earth,—gave token of the glorious Northern spring, the rapid, fleeting joy of that most melancholy of Natures. The wind was beginning to lift the veil of mist which half-obscured the gulf. The birds sang. The bark of the trees where the sun had not yet dried the clinging hoar-frost shone gayly to the eye in its fantastic wreathings which trickled away in murmuring rivulets as the warmth reached them. The three friends walked in silence along the shore. Wilfrid and Minna alone noticed the magic transformation that was taking place in the monotonous picture of the winter landscape. Their companion walked in thought, as though a voice were sounding to her ears in this concert of Nature.

Presently they reached the ledge of rocks through which the Sieg had forced its way, after escaping from the long avenue cut by its waters in an undulating line through the forest,—a fluvial pathway flanked by aged firs and roofed with strong-ribbed arches like those of a cathedral. Looking back from that vantage-ground, the whole extent of the fiord could be seen at a glance, with the open sea sparkling on the horizon beyond it like a burnished blade.

At this moment the mist, rolling away, left the sky blue and clear. Among the valleys and around the trees flitted the shining fragments,—a diamond dust swept by the freshening breeze. The torrent rolled on toward them; along its length a vapor rose, tinted by the sun with every color of his light; the decomposing rays flashing prismatic fires along the many-tinted scarf of waters. The rugged ledge on which they stood was carpeted by several kinds of lichen, forming a noble mat variegated by moisture and lustrous like the sheen of a silken fabric. Shrubs, already in bloom, crowned the rocks with garlands. Their waving foliage, eager for the freshness of the water, drooped its tresses above the stream; the larches shook their light fringes and played with the pines, stiff and motionless as aged men. This luxuriant beauty was foiled by the solemn colonnades of the forest-trees, rising in terraces upon the mountains, and by the calm sheet of the fiord, lying below, where the torrent buried its fury and was still. Beyond, the sea hemmed in this page of Nature, written by the greatest of poets, Chance; to whom the wild luxuriance of creation when apparently abandoned to itself is owing.

The village of Jarvis was a lost point in the landscape, in this immensity of Nature, sublime at this moment like all things else of ephemeral life which present a fleeting image of perfection; for, by a law fatal to no eyes but our own, creations which appear complete—the love of our heart and the desire of our eyes—have but one spring-tide here below. Standing on this breast-work of rock these three persons might well suppose themselves alone in the universe.

"What beauty!" cried Wilfrid.

"Nature sings hymns," said Seraphita. "Is not her music exquisite? Tell me, Wilfrid, could any of the women you once knew create such a glorious retreat for herself as this? I am conscious here of a feeling seldom inspired by the sight of cities, a longing to lie down amid this quickening verdure. Here, with eyes to heaven and an open heart, lost in the bosom of immensity, I could hear the sighings of the flower, scarce budded, which longs for wings, or the cry of the eider grieving that it can only fly, and remember the desires of man who, issuing from all, is none the less ever longing. But that, Wilfrid, is only a woman's thought. You find seductive fancies in the wreathing mists, the light embroidered veils which Nature dons like a coy maiden, in this atmosphere where she perfumes for her spousals the greenery of her tresses. You seek the naiad's form amid the gauzy vapors, and to your thinking my ears should listen only to the virile voice of the Torrent."

"But Love is there, like the bee in the calyx of the flower," replied Wilfrid, perceiving for the first time a trace of earthly sentiment in her words, and fancying the moment favorable for an expression of his passionate tenderness.

"Always there?" said Seraphita, smiling. Minna had left them for a moment to gather the blue saxifrages growing on a rock above.

"Always," repeated Wilfrid. "Hear me," he said, with a

masterful glance which was foiled as by a diamond breast-plate. "You know not what I am, nor what I can be, nor what I will. Do not reject my last entreaty. Be mine for the good of that world whose happiness you bear upon your heart. Be mine that my conscience may be pure; that a voice divine may sound in my ears and infuse Good into the great enterprise I have undertaken prompted by my hatred to the nations, but which I swear to accomplish for their benefit if you will walk beside me. What higher mission can you ask for love? what nobler part can woman aspire to? I came to Norway to meditate a grand design."

"And you will sacrifice its grandeur," she said, "to an innocent girl who loves you, and who will lead you in the paths of peace."

"What matters sacrifice," he cried, "if I have you? Hear my secret. I have gone from end to end of the North,—that great smithy from whose anvils new races have spread over the earth, like human tides appointed to refresh the wornout civilizations. I wished to begin my work at some Northern point, to win the empire which force and intellect must ever give over a primitive people; to form that people for battle, to drive them to wars which should ravage Europe like a conflagration, crying liberty to some, pillage to others, glory here, pleasure there!—I, myself, remaining an image of Destiny, cruel, implacable, advancing like the whirlwind, which sucks from the atmosphere the particles that make the thunderbolt, and falls like a devouring scourge upon the nations. Europe is at an epoch when she awaits the new Messiah who shall destroy society and remake it. She can no longer believe except in him who crushes her under foot. The day is at hand when poets and historians will justify me, exalt me, and borrow my ideas, mine! And all the while my triumph will be a jest, written in blood, the jest of my vengeance! But not here, Seraphita; what I see in the North disgusts me. Hers is a mere blind force; I thirst for the Indies! I would rather fight a selfish, cowardly, mercantile government. Besides, it is easier to stir the imagination of the peoples at the feet of the Caucasus than to argue with the intellect of the icy lands which here surround me. Therefore am I tempted to cross the Russian steps and pour my triumphant human tide through Asia to the Ganges, and overthrow the British rule. Seven men have done this thing before me in other epochs of the world. I will emulate them. I will spread Art like the Saracens, hurled by Mohammed upon Europe. Mine shall be no paltry sovereignty like those that govern to-day the ancient provinces of the Roman empire, disputing with their subjects about a customs right! No, nothing can bar my way! Like Genghis Khan, my feet shall tread a third of the globe, my hand shall grasp the throat of Asia like Aurung-Zeb. Be my companion! Let me seat thee, beautiful and noble being, on a throne! I do not doubt success, but live within my heart and I am sure of it."

"I have already reigned," said Seraphita, coldly.

The words fell as the axe of a skilful woodman falls at the root of a young tree and brings it down at a single blow. Men alone can comprehend the rage that a woman excites in the soul of a man when, after showing her his strength, his power, his wisdom, his superiority, the capricious creature bends her head and says, "All that is nothing"; when, unmoved, she smiles and says, "Such things are known to me," as though his power were nought.

"What!" cried Wilfrid, in despair, "can the riches of art, the riches of worlds, the splendors of a court—"

She stopped him by a single inflexion of her lips, and said, "Beings more powerful than you have offered me far more."

"Thou hast no soul," he cried,—"no soul, if thou art not persuaded by the thought of comforting a great man, who is willing now to sacrifice all things to live beside thee in a little house on the shores of a lake."

"But," she said, "I am loved with a boundless love."

"By whom?" cried Wilfrid, approaching Seraphita with a frenzied movement, as if to fling her into the foaming basin of the Sieg.

She looked at him and slowly extended her arm, pointing to Minna, who now sprang towards her, fair and glowing and lovely as the flowers she held in her hand.

"Child!" said Seraphitus, advancing to meet her.

Wilfrid remained where she left him, motionless as the rock on which he stood, lost in thought, longing to let himself go into the torrent of the Sieg, like the fallen trees which hurried past his eyes and disappeared in the bosom of the gulf.

"I gathered them for you," said Minna, offering the bunch of saxifrages to the being she adored. "One of them, see, this one," she added, selecting a flower, "is like that you found on the Falberg."

Seraphitus looked alternately at the flower and at Minna.

"Why question me? Dost thou doubt me?"

"No," said the young girl, "my trust in you is infinite. You are more beautiful to look upon than this glorious nature, but your mind surpasses in intellect that of all humanity. When I have been with you I seem to have prayed to God. I long—"

"For what?" said Seraphitus, with a glance that revealed to the young girl the vast distance which separated them.

"To suffer in your stead."

"Ah, dangerous being!" cried Seraphitus in his heart. "Is it wrong, oh my God! to desire to offer her to Thee? Dost thou remember, Minna, what I said to thee up there?" he added, pointing to the summit of the Ice-Cap.

"He is terrible again," thought Minna, trembling with fear.

The voice of the Sieg accompanied the thoughts of the three beings united on this platform of projecting rock, but separated in soul by the abysses of the Spiritual World.

"Seraphitus! teach me," said Minna in a silvery voice, soft as the motion of a sensitive plant, "teach me how to cease to love you. Who could fail to admire you; love is an admiration that never wearies."

"Poor child!" said Seraphitus, turning pale; "there is but one whom thou canst love in that way."

"Who?" asked Minna.

"Thou shalt know hereafter," he said, in the feeble voice of a man who lies down to die.

"Help, help! he is dying!" cried Minna.

Wilfrid ran towards them. Seeing Seraphita as she lay on a fragment of gneiss, where time had cast its velvet mantle of lustrous lichen and tawny mosses now burnished in the sunlight, he whispered softly, "How beautiful she is!"

"One other look! the last that I shall ever cast upon this nature in travail," said Seraphitus, rallying her strength and rising to her feet.

She advanced to the edge of the rocky platform, whence her eyes took in the scenery of that grand and glorious landscape, so verdant, flowery, and animated, yet so lately buried in its winding-sheet of snow.

"Farewell," she said, "farewell, home of Earth, warmed by the fires of Love; where all things press with ardent force from the centre to the extremities; where the extremities are gathered up, like a woman's hair, to weave the mysterious braid which binds us in that invisible ether to the Thought Divine!

"Behold the man bending above that furrow moistened with his tears, who lifts his head for an instant to question Heaven; behold the woman gathering her children that she may feed them with her milk; see him who lashes the ropes in the height of the gale; see her who sits in the hollow of the rocks, awaiting the father! Behold all they who stretch their hands in want after a lifetime spent in thankless toil. To all peace and courage, and to all farewell!

"Hear you the cry of the soldier, dying nameless and unknown? the wail of the man deceived who weeps in the desert? To them peace and courage; to all farewell!

"Farewell, you who die for the kings of the earth! Farewell, ye people without a country and ye countries without a people, each, with a mutual want. Above all, farewell to Thee who knew not where to lay Thy head, Exile divine! Farewell, mothers beside your dying sons! Farewell, ye Little Ones, ye Feeble, ye Suffering, you whose sorrows I have so often borne! Farewell, all ye who have descended into the sphere of Instinct that you may suffer there for others!

"Farewell, ye mariners who seek the Orient through the thick darkness of your abstractions, vast as principles! Farewell, martyrs of thought, led by thought into the presence of the True Light. Farewell, regions of study where mine ears can hear the plaint of genius neglected and insulted, the sigh of the patient scholar to whom enlightenment comes too late!

"I see the angelic choir, the wafting of perfumes, the incense of the heart of those who go their way consoling, praying, imparting celestial balm and living light to suffering souls! Courage, ye choir of Love! you to whom the peoples cry, 'Comfort us, comfort us, defend us!' To you courage! and farewell!

"Farewell, ye granite rocks that shall bloom a flower; farewell, flower that becomes a dove; farewell, dove that shalt be woman; farewell, woman, who art Suffering, man, who art Belief! Farewell, you who shall be all love, all prayer!"

Broken with fatigue, this inexplicable being leaned for the first time on Wilfrid and on Minna to be taken home. Wilfrid and Minna felt the shock of a mysterious contact in and through the being who thus connected them. They had scarcely advanced a few steps when David met them, weeping. "She will die," he said, "why have you brought her hither?"

The old man raised her in his arms with the vigor of youth and bore her to the gate of the Swedish castle like an eagle bearing a white lamb to his mountain eyrie.

CHAPTER VI

THE PATH TO HEAVEN

The day succeeding that on which Seraphita foresaw her death and bade farewell to Earth, as a prisoner looks round his dungeon before leaving it forever, she suffered pains which obliged her to remain in the helpless immobility of those whose pangs are great. Wilfrid and Minna went to see her, and found her lying on her couch of furs. Still veiled in flesh, her soul shone through that veil, which grew more and more transparent day by day. The progress of the Spirit, piercing the last obstacle between itself and the Infinite, was called an illness, the hour of Life went by the name of death. David wept as he watched her sufferings; unreasonable as a child, he would not listen to his mistress's consolations. Monsieur Becker wished Seraphita to try remedies; but all were useless.

One morning she sent for the two beings whom she loved, telling them that this would be the last of her bad days. Wilfrid and Minna came in terror, knowing well that they were about to lose her. Seraphita smiled to them as one departing to a better world; her head drooped like a flower heavy with dew, which opens its calyx for the last time to waft its fragrance on the breeze. She looked at these friends with a sadness that was for them, not for herself; she thought no longer of herself, and they felt this with a grief mingled with gratitude which they were unable to express. Wilfrid stood silent and motionless, lost in thoughts excited by events whose vast bearings enabled him to conceive of some illimitable immensity.

Emboldened by the weakness of the being lately so powerful, or perhaps by the fear of losing him forever, Minna bent down over the couch and said, "Seraphitus, let me follow thee!"

"Can I forbid thee?"

"Why will thou not love me enough to stay with me?"

"I can love nothing here."

115

"What canst thou love?"

"Heaven."

"Is it worthy of heaven to despise the creatures of God?"

"Minna, can we love two beings at once? Would our beloved be indeed our beloved if he did not fill our hearts? Must he not be the first, the last, the only one? She who is all love, must she not leave the world for her beloved? Human ties are but a memory, she has no ties except to him! Her soul is hers no longer; it is his. If she keeps within her soul anything that is not his, does she love? No, she loves not. To love feebly, is that to love at all? The voice of her beloved makes her joyful; it flows through her veins in a crimson tide more glowing far than blood; his glance is the light that penetrates her; her being melts into his being. He is warm to her soul. He is the light that lightens; near to him there is neither cold nor darkness. He is never absent, he is always with us; we think in him, to him, by him! Minna, that is how I love him."

"Love whom?" said Minna, tortured with sudden jealousy.

"God," replied Seraphitus, his voice glowing in their souls like fires of liberty from peak to peak upon the mountains,—"God, who does not betray us! God, who will never abandon us! who crowns our wishes; who satisfies His creatures with joy—joy unalloyed and infinite! God, who never wearies but ever smiles! God, who pours into the soul fresh treasures day by day; who purifies and leaves no bitterness; who is all harmony, all flame! God, who has placed Himself within our hearts to blossom there; who hearkens to our prayers; who does not stand aloof when we are His, but gives His presence absolutely! He who revives us, magnifies us, and multiplies us in Himself; God! Minna, I love thee because thou mayst be His! I love thee because if thou come to Him thou wilt be mine."

"Lead me to Him," cried Minna, kneeling down; "take me by the hand; I will not leave thee!"

"Lead us, Seraphita!" cried Wilfrid, coming to Minna's side with an impetuous movement. "Yes, thou hast given me a thirst for Light, a thirst for the Word. I am parched with the Love thou hast put into my heart; I desire to keep thy soul in mine; thy will is mine; I will do whatsoever thou biddest me. Since I cannot obtain thee, I will keep thy will and all the thoughts that thou hast given me. If I may not unite myself with thee except by the power of my spirit, I will cling to thee in soul as the flame to what it laps. Speak!"

"Angel!" exclaimed the mysterious being, enfolding them both in one glance, as it were with an azure mantle, "Heaven shall by thine heritage!"

Silence fell among them after these words, which sounded in the souls of the man and of the woman like the first notes of some celestial harmony.

"If you would teach your feet to tread the Path to heaven, know that the way is hard at first," said the weary sufferer; "God wills that you shall seek Him for Himself. In that sense, He is jealous; He demands your whole self. But when you have given Him yourself, never, never will He abandon you. I leave with you the keys of the kingdom of His Light, where evermore you shall dwell in the bosom of the Father, in the heart of the Bridegroom. No sentinels guard the approaches, you may enter where you will; His palaces, His treasures, His sceptre, all are free. 'Take them!' He says. But—you must will to go there. Like one preparing for a journey, a man must leave his home, renounce his projects, bid farewell to friends, to father, mother, sister, even to the helpless brother who cries after him,—yes, farewell to them eternally; you will no more return than did the martyrs on their way to the stake. You must strip yourself of every sentiment, of everything to which man clings. Unless you do this you are but half-hearted in your enterprise.

"Do for God what you do for your ambitious projects, what you do in consecrating yourself to Art, what you have done when you loved a human creature or sought some secret of human science. Is not God the whole of science, the all of love, the source of poetry? Surely His riches are worthy of being coveted! His treasure is inexhaustible, His poem infinite, His love immutable, His science sure and darkened by no mysteries. Be anxious for nothing, He will give you all. Yes, in His heart are treasures with which the petty joys you lose on earth are not to be compared. What I tell you is true; you shall possess His power; you may use it as you would use the gifts of lover or mistress. Alas! men doubt, they lack faith, and will, and persistence. If some set their feet in the path, they look behind them and presently turn back. Few decide between the two extremes,—to go or stay, heaven or the mire. All hesitate. Weakness leads astray, passion allures into dangerous paths, vice becomes habitual, man flounders in the mud and makes no progress towards a better state.

"All human beings go through a previous life in the sphere of Instinct, where they are brought to see the worthlessness of earthly treasures, to amass which they gave themselves such untold pains! Who can tell how many times the human being lives in the sphere of Instinct before he is prepared to enter the sphere of Abstractions, where thought expends itself on erring science, where mind wearies at last of human language? for, when Matter is exhausted, Spirit enters. Who knows how many fleshly forms the heir of heaven occupies before he can be brought to understand the value of that silence and solitude whose starry plains are but the vestibule of Spiritual Worlds? He feels his way amid the void, makes trial of nothingness, and then at last his eyes revert upon the Path. Then follow other existences,—all to be lived to reach the place where Light effulgent shines. Death is the post-house of the journey. A lifetime may be needed merely to gain the virtues which annul the errors of man's preceding life. First comes the life of suffering, whose tortures create a thirst for love. Next the life of love and devotion to the creature, teaching devotion to the Creator,—a life where the virtues of love, its martyrdoms, its joys followed by sorrows, its angelic hopes, its patience, its resignation, excite an appetite for things divine. Then follows the life which seeks in silence the traces of the Word; in which the soul grows humble and charitable. Next the life of longing; and lastly, the life of prayer. In that is the noonday sun; there are the flowers, there the harvest!

"The virtues we acquire, which develop slowly within us, are the invisible links that bind each one of our existences to the others,—existences which the spirit alone remembers, for Matter has no memory for spiritual things. Thought alone holds the tradition of the bygone life. The endless legacy of the past to the present is the secret source of human genius. Some receive the gift of form, some the gift of numbers, others the gift of harmony. All these gifts are steps of progress in the Path of Light. Yes, he who possesses a single one of them touches at that point the Infinite. Earth has divided the Word—of which I here reveal some syllables—into particles, she has reduced it to dust and has scattered it through her works, her dogmas, her poems. If some impalpable grain shines like a diamond in a human work, men cry: 'How grand! how true! how glorious!' That fragment vibrates in their souls and wakes a presentiment of heaven: to some, a melody that weans from earth; to others, the solitude that draws to God. To all, whatsoever sends us back upon ourselves, whatsoever strikes us down and crushes us, lifts or abases us,—that is but a syllable of the Divine Word.

"When a human soul draws its first furrow straight, the rest will follow surely. One thought borne inward, one prayer uplifted, one suffering endured, one echo of the Word within us, and our souls are forever changed. All ends in God; and many are the ways to find Him by walking straight before us. When the happy day arrives in which you set your feet upon the Path and begin your pilgrimage, the world will know nothing of it; earth no longer understands you; you no longer understand each other. Men who attain a knowledge of these things, who lisp a few syllables of the Word, often have not where to lay their head; hunted like beasts they perish on the scaffold, to the joy of assembled peoples, while Angels open to them the gates of heaven. Therefore, your destiny is a secret between yourself and God, just as love is a secret between two hearts. You may be the buried treasure, trodden under the feet of men thirsting for gold yet all-unknowing that you are there beneath them.

"Henceforth your existence becomes a thing of ceaseless activity; each act has a meaning which connects you with God, just as in love your actions and your thoughts are filled with the loved one. But love and its joys, love and its pleasures limited by the senses, are but the imperfect image of the love which unites you to your celestial Spouse. All earthly joy is mixed with anguish, with discontent. If love ought not to pall then death should end it while its flame is high, so that we see no ashes. But in God our wretchedness becomes delight, joy lives upon itself and multiplies, and grows, and has no limit. In the Earthly life our fleeting love is ended by tribulation; in the Spiritual life the tribulations of a day end in joys unending. The soul is ceaselessly joyful. We feel God with us, in us; He gives a sacred savor to all things; He shines in the soul; He imparts to us His sweetness; He stills our interest in the world viewed for ourselves; He quickens our interest in it viewed for His sake, and grants us the exercise of His power upon it. In His name we do the works which He inspires, we act for Him, we have no self except in Him, we love His creatures with undying love, we dry their tears and long to bring them unto Him, as a loving woman longs to see the inhabitants of earth obey her well-beloved.

"The final life, the fruition of all other lives, to which the powers of the soul have tended, and whose merits open the Sacred Portals to perfected man, is the life of Prayer. Who can make you comprehend the grandeur, the majesty, the might of Prayer? May my voice, these words of mine, ring in your hearts and change them. Be now, here, what you may be after cruel trial! There are privileged beings, Prophets, Seers, Messengers, and Martyrs, all those who suffer for the Word and who proclaim it; such souls spring at a bound across the human sphere and rise at once to Prayer. So, too, with those whose souls receive the fire of Faith. Be one of those brave souls! God welcomes boldness. He loves to be taken by violence; He will never reject those who force their way to Him. Know this! desire, the torrent of your will, is so all-powerful that a single emission of it, made with force, can obtain all; a single cry, uttered under the pressure of Faith, suffices. Be one of such beings, full of force, of will, of love! Be conquerors on the earth! Let the hunger and thirst of God possess you. Fly to Him as the hart panting for the water-brooks. Desire shall lend you its wings; tears, those blossoms of repentance, shall be the celestial baptism from which your nature will issue purified. Cast yourself on the breast of the stream in Prayer! Silence and meditation are the means of following the Way. God reveals Himself, unfailingly, to the solitary, thoughtful seeker.

"It is thus that the separation takes place between Matter, which so long has wrapped its darkness round you, and Spirit, which was in you from the beginning, the light which lighted you and now brings noon-day to your soul. Yes, your broken heart shall receive the light; the light shall bathe it. Then you will no longer feel convictions, they will have changed to certainties. The Poet utters; the Thinker meditates; the Righteous acts; but he who stands upon the borders of the Divine World prays; and his prayer is word, thought, action, in one! Yes, prayer includes all, contains all; it completes nature, for it reveals to you the mind within it and its progression. White and shining virgin of all human virtues, ark of the covenant between earth and heaven, tender and strong companion partaking of the lion and of the lamb, Prayer! Prayer will give you the key of heaven! Bold and pure as innocence, strong, like all that is single and simple, this glorious, invincible Queen rests, nevertheless, on the material world; she takes possession of it; like the sun, she clasps it in a circle of light. The universe belongs to him who wills, who knows, who prays; but he must will, he must know, he must pray; in a word, he must possess force, wisdom, and faith.

"Therefore Prayer, issuing from so many trials, is the consummation of all truths, all powers, all feelings. Fruit of the laborious, progressive, continued development of natural properties and faculties vitalized anew by the divine breath of the Word, Prayer has occult activity; it is the final worship—not the material worship of images, nor the spiritual worship of formulas, but the worship of the Divine World. We say no prayers,—prayer forms within us; it is a faculty which acts of itself; it has attained a way of action which lifts it outside of forms; it links the soul to God, with whom we unite as the root of the tree unites with the soil; our veins draw life from the principle of life, and we live by the life of the universe. Prayer bestows external conviction by making us penetrate the Material World through the cohesion of all our faculties with the elementary substances; it bestows internal conviction by developing our essence and mingling it with that of the Spiritual Worlds. To be able to pray thus, you must attain to an utter abandonment of flesh; you must acquire through the fires of the furnace the purity of the diamond; for this complete communion with the Divine is obtained only in absolute repose, where storms and conflicts are at rest.

"Yes, Prayer—the aspiration of the soul freed absolutely from the body—bears all forces within it, and applies them to the constant and perseverant union of the Visible and the Invisible. When you possess the faculty of praying without weariness, with love, with force, with certainty, with intelligence, your spiritualized nature will presently be invested with power. Like a rushing wind, like a thunderbolt, it cuts its way through all things and shares the power of God. The quickness of the Spirit becomes yours; in an instant you may pass from region to region; like the Word itself, you are transported from the ends of the world to other worlds. Harmony exists, and you are part of it! Light is there and your eyes possess it! Melody is heard and you echo it! Under such conditions, you feel your perceptions developing, widening; the eyes of your mind reach to vast distances. There is, in truth, neither time nor place to the Spirit; space and duration are proportions created for Matter; spirit and matter have naught in common.

"Though these things take place in stillness, in silence, without agitation, without external movement, yet Prayer is all action; but it is spiritual action, stripped of substantiality, and reduced, like the motion of the worlds, to an invisible pure force. It penetrates everywhere like light; it gives vitality to souls that come beneath its rays, as Nature beneath the sun. It resuscitates virtue, purifies and sanctifies all actions, peoples solitude, and gives a foretaste of eternal joys. When you have once felt the delights of the divine intoxication which comes of this internal travail, then all is yours! once take the lute on which we sing to God within your hands, and you will never part with it. Hence the solitude in which Angelic Spirits live; hence their disdain of human joys. They are withdrawn from those who must die to live; they hear the language of such beings, but they no longer understand their ideas; they wonder at their movements, at what the world terms policies, material laws, societies. For them all mysteries are over; truth, and truth alone, is theirs. They who have reached the point where their eyes discern the Sacred Portals, who, not looking back, not uttering one regret, contemplate worlds and comprehend their destinies, such as they keep silence, wait, and bear their final struggles. The worst of all those struggles is the last; at the zenith of all virtue is Resignation,—

to be an exile and not lament, no longer to delight in earthly things and yet to smile, to belong to God and yet to stay with men! You hear the voice that cries to you, 'Advance!' Often celestial visions of descending Angels compass you about with songs of praise; then, tearless, uncomplaining, must you watch them as they reascent the skies! To murmur is to forfeit all. Resignation is a fruit that ripens at the gates of heaven. How powerful, how glorious the calm smile, the pure brow of the resigned human creature. Radiant is the light of that brow. They who live in its atmosphere grow purer. That calm glance penetrates and softens. More eloquent by silence than the prophet by speech, such beings triumph by their simple presence. Their ears are quick to hear as a faithful dog listening for his master. Brighter than hope, stronger than love, higher than faith, that creature of resignation is the virgin standing on the earth, who holds for a moment the conquered palm, then, rising heavenward, leaves behind her the imprint of her white, pure feet. When she has passed away men flock around and cry, 'See! See!' Sometimes God holds her still in sight,—a figure to whose feet creep Forms and Species of Animality to be shown their way. She wafts the light exhaling from her hair, and they see; she speaks, and they hear. 'A miracle!' they cry. Often she triumphs in the name of God; frightened men deny her and put her to death; smiling, she lays down her sword and goes to the stake, having saved the Peoples. How many a pardoned Angel has passed from martyrdom to heaven! Sinai, Golgotha are not in this place nor in that; Angels are crucified in every place, in every sphere. Sighs pierce to God from the whole universe. This earth on which we live is but a single sheaf of the great harvest; humanity is but a species in the vast garden where the flowers of heaven are cultivated. Everywhere God is like unto Himself, and everywhere, by prayer, it is easy to reach Him."

With these words, which fell from the lips of another Hagar in the wilderness, burning the souls of the hearers as the live coal of the word inflamed Isaiah, this mysterious being paused as though to gather some remaining strength. Wilfrid and Minna dared not speak. Suddenly HE lifted himself up to die:—

"Soul of all things, oh my God, thou whom I love for Thyself!

Thou, Judge and Father, receive a love which has no limit. Give me of thine essence and thy faculties that I be wholly thine! Take me, that I no longer be myself! Am I not purified? then cast me back into the furnace! If I be not yet proved in the fire, make me some nurturing ploughshare, or the Sword of victory! Grant me a glorious martyrdom in which to proclaim thy Word! Rejected, I will bless thy justice. But if excess of love may win in a moment that which hard and patient labor cannot attain, then bear me upward in thy chariot of fire! Grant me triumph, or further trial, still will I bless thee! To suffer for thee, is not that to triumph? Take me, seize me, bear me away! nay, if thou wilt, reject me! Thou art He who can do no evil. Ah!" he cried, after a pause, "the bonds are breaking.

"Spirits of the pure, ye sacred flock, come forth from the hidden places, come on the surface of the luminous waves! The hour now is; come, assemble! Let us sing at the gates of the Sanctuary; our songs shall drive away the final clouds. With one accord let us hail the Dawn of the Eternal Day. Behold the rising of the one True Light! Ah, why may I not take with me these my friends! Farewell, poor earth, Farewell!"

CHAPTER VII

THE ASSUMPTION

The last psalm was uttered neither by word, look, nor gesture, nor by any of those signs which men employ to communicate their thoughts, but as the soul speaks to itself; for at the moment when Seraphita revealed herself in her true nature, her thoughts were no longer enslaved by human words. The violence of that last prayer had burst her bonds. Her soul, like a white dove, remained for an instant poised above the body whose exhausted substances were about to be annihilated.

The aspiration of the Soul toward heaven was so contagious that Wilfrid and Minna, beholding those radiant scintillations of Life, perceived not Death.

They had fallen on their knees when he had turned toward his Orient, and they shared his ecstasy.

The fear of the Lord, which creates man a second time, purging away his dross, mastered their hearts.

Their eyes, veiled to the things of Earth, were opened to the Brightness of Heaven.

Though, like the Seers of old called Prophets by men, they were filled with the terror of the Most High, yet like them they continued firm when they found themselves within the radiance where the Glory of the Spirit shone.

The veil of flesh, which, until now, had hidden that glory from their eyes, dissolved imperceptibly away, and left them free to behold the Divine substance.

They stood in the twilight of the Coming Dawn, whose feeble rays prepared them to look upon the True Light, to hear the Living Word, and yet not die.

In this state they began to perceive the immeasurable differences which separate the things of earth from the things of Heaven.

Life, on the borders of which they stood, leaning upon each other, trembling and illuminated, like two children standing under shelter in presence of a conflagration, That Life offered no lodgment to the senses.

The ideas they used to interpret their vision to themselves were to the things seen what the visible senses of a man are to his soul, the material covering of a divine essence.

The departing spirit was above them, shedding incense without odor, melody without sound. About them, where they stood, were neither surfaces, nor angles, nor atmosphere.

They dared neither question him nor contemplate him; they stood in the shadow of that Presence as beneath the burning rays of a tropical sun, fearing to raise their eyes lest the light should blast them.

They knew they were beside him, without being able to perceive how it was that they stood, as in a dream, on the confines of the Visible and the Invisible, nor how they had lost sight of the Visible and how they beheld the Invisible.

To each other they said: "If he touches us, we can die!" But the spirit was now within the Infinite, and they knew not that neither time, nor space, nor death, existed there, and that a great gulf lay between them, although they thought themselves beside him.

Their souls were not prepared to receive in its fulness a knowledge of the faculties of that Life; they could have only faint and confused perceptions of it, suited to their weakness.

Were it not so, the thunder of the Living Word, whose far-off tones now reached their ears, and whose meaning entered their souls as life unites with body,—one echo of that Word would have consumed their being as a whirlwind of fire laps up a fragile straw.

Therefore they saw only that which their nature, sustained by the strength of the spirit, permitted them to see; they heard that only which they were able to hear.

And yet, though thus protected, they shuddered when the Voice of the anguished soul broke forth above them—the prayer of the Spirit awaiting Life and imploring it with a cry.

That cry froze them to the very marrow of their bones.

The Spirit knocked at the sacred portal. "What wilt thou?"

answered a choir, whose question echoed among the worlds. "To go to God." "Hast thou conquered?" "I have conquered the flesh through abstinence, I have conquered false knowledge by humility, I have conquered pride by charity, I have conquered the earth by love; I have paid my dues by suffering, I am purified in the fires of faith, I have longed for Life by prayer: I wait in adoration, and I am resigned."

No answer came.

"God's will be done!" answered the Spirit, believing that he was about to be rejected.

His tears flowed and fell like dew upon the heads of the two kneeling witnesses, who trembled before the justice of God.

Suddenly the trumpets sounded,—the last trumpets of Victory won by the Angel in this last trial. The reverberation passed through space as sound through its echo, filling it, and shaking the universe which Wilfrid and Minna felt like an atom beneath their feet. They trembled under an anguish caused by the dread of the mystery about to be accomplished.

A great movement took place, as though the Eternal Legions, putting themselves in motion, were passing upward in spiral columns. The worlds revolved like clouds driven by a furious wind. It was all rapid.

Suddenly the veils were rent away. They saw on high as it were a star, incomparably more lustrous than the most luminous of material stars, which detached itself, and fell like a thunderbolt, dazzling as lightning. Its passage paled the faces of the pair, who thought it to be the Light Itself.

It was the Messenger of good tidings, the plume of whose helmet was a flame of Life.

Behind him lay the swath of his way gleaming with a flood of the lights through which he passed.

He bore a palm and a sword. He touched the Spirit with the palm, and the Spirit was transfigured. Its white wings noiselessly unfolded.

This communication of the Light, changing the Spirit into a Seraph and clothing it with a glorious form, a celestial armor, poured down such effulgent rays that the two Seers were paralyzed.

Like the three apostles to whom Jesus showed himself, they felt the dead weight of their bodies which denied them a complete and cloudless intuition of the Word and the True Life.

They comprehended the nakedness of their souls; they were able to measure the poverty of their light by comparing it—a humbling task—with the halo of the Seraph.

A passionate desire to plunge back into the mire of earth and suffer trial took possession of them,—trial through which they might victoriously utter at the sacred gates the words of that radiant Seraph.

The Seraph knelt before the Sanctuary, beholding it, at last, face to face; and he said, raising his hands thitherward, "Grant that these two may have further sight; they will love the Lord and proclaim His word."

At this prayer a veil fell. Whether it were that the hidden force which held the Seers had momentarily annihilated their physical bodies, or that it raised their spirits above those bodies, certain it is that they felt within them a rending of the pure from the impure.

The tears of the Seraph rose about them like a vapor, which hid the lower worlds from their knowledge, held them in its folds, bore them upwards, gave them forgetfulness of earthly meanings and the power of comprehending the meanings of things divine.

The True Light shone; it illumined the Creations, which seemed to them barren when they saw the source from which all worlds—Terrestrial, Spiritual, and Divine-derived their Motion.

Each world possessed a centre to which converged all points of its circumference. These worlds were themselves the points which moved toward the centre of their system. Each system had its centre in great celestial regions which communicated with the flaming and quenchless motor of all that is.

Thus, from the greatest to the smallest of the worlds, and from the smallest of the worlds to the smallest portion of the beings who compose it, all was individual, and all was, nevertheless, One and indivisible.

What was the design of the Being, fixed in His essence and in

His faculties, who transmitted that essence and those faculties without losing them? who manifested them outside of Himself without separating them from Himself? who rendered his creations outside of Himself fixed in their essence and mutable in their form? The pair thus called to the celestial festival could only see the order and arrangement of created beings and admire the immediate result. The Angels alone see more. They know the means; they comprehend the final end.

But what the two Elect were granted power to contemplate, what they were able to bring back as a testimony which enlightened their minds forever after, was the proof of the action of the Worlds and of Beings; the consciousness of the effort with which they all converge to the Result.

They heard the divers parts of the Infinite forming one living melody; and each time that the accord made itself felt like a mighty respiration, the Worlds drawn by the concordant movement inclined themselves toward the Supreme Being who, from His impenetrable centre, issued all things and recalled all things to Himself.

This ceaseless alternation of voices and silence seemed the rhythm of the sacred hymn which resounds and prolongs its sound from age to age.

Wilfrid and Minna were enabled to understand some of the mysterious sayings of Him who had appeared on earth in the form which to each of them had rendered him comprehensible,—to one Seraphitus, to the other Seraphita,—for they saw that all was homogeneous in the sphere where he now was.

Light gave birth to melody, melody gave birth to light; colors were light and melody; motion was a Number endowed with Utterance; all things were at once sonorous, diaphanous, and mobile; so that each interpenetrated the other, the whole vast area was unobstructed and the Angels could survey it from the depths of the Infinite.

They perceived the puerility of human sciences, of which he had spoken to them.

The scene was to them a prospect without horizon, a boundless space into which an all-consuming desire prompted them to plunge. But, fastened to their miserable bodies, they had the desire without the power to fulfil it.

The Seraph, preparing for his flight, no longer looked towards them; he had nothing now in common with Earth.

Upward he rose; the shadow of his luminous presence covered the two Seers like a merciful veil, enabling them to raise their eyes and see him, rising in his glory to Heaven in company with the glad Archangel.

He rose as the sun from the bosom of the Eastern waves; but, more majestic than the orb and vowed to higher destinies, he could not be enchained like inferior creations in the spiral movement of the worlds; he followed the line of the Infinite, pointing without deviation to the One Centre, there to enter his eternal life,—to receive there, in his faculties and in his essence, the power to enjoy through Love, and the gift of comprehending through Wisdom.

The scene which suddenly unveiled itself to the eyes of the two Seers crushed them with a sense of its vastness; they felt like atoms, whose minuteness was not to be compared even to the smallest particle which the infinite of divisibility enabled the mind of man to imagine, brought into the presence of the infinite of Numbers, which God alone can comprehend as He alone can comprehend Himself.

Strength and Love! what heights, what depths in those two entities, whom the Seraph's first prayer placed like two links, as it were, to unite the immensities of the lower worlds with the immensity of the higher universe!

They comprehended the invisible ties by which the material worlds are bound to the spiritual worlds. Remembering the sublime efforts of human genius, they were able to perceive the principle of all melody in the songs of heaven which gave sensations of color, of perfume, of thought, which recalled the innumerable details of all creations, as the songs of earth revive the infinite memories of love.

Brought by the exaltation of their faculties to a point that cannot be described in any language, they were able to cast their eyes for an instant into the Divine World. There all was Rejoicing.

Myriads of angels were flocking together, without confusion;

all alike yet all dissimilar, simple as the flower of the fields, majestic as the universe.

Wilfrid and Minna saw neither their coming nor their going; they appeared suddenly in the Infinite and filled it with their presence, as the stars shine in the invisible ether.

The scintillations of their united diadems illumined space like the fires of the sky at dawn upon the mountains. Waves of light flowed from their hair, and their movements created tremulous undulations in space like the billows of a phosphorescent sea.

The two Seers beheld the Seraph dimly in the midst of the immortal legions. Suddenly, as though all the arrows of a quiver had darted together, the Spirits swept away with a breath the last vestiges of the human form; as the Seraph rose he became yet purer; soon he seemed to them but a faint outline of what he had been at the moment of his transfiguration,—lines of fire without shadow.

Higher he rose, receiving from circle to circle some new gift, while the sign of his election was transmitted to each sphere into which, more and more purified, he entered.

No voice was silent; the hymn diffused and multiplied itself in all its modulations:—

"Hail to him who enters living! Come, flower of the Worlds! diamond from the fires of suffering! pearl without spot, desire without flesh, new link of earth and heaven, be Light! Conquering spirit, Queen of the world, come for thy crown! Victor of earth, receive thy diadem! Thou art of us!"

The virtues of the Seraph shone forth in all their beauty.

His earliest desire for heaven re-appeared, tender as childhood. The deeds of his life, like constellations, adorned him with their brightness. His acts of faith shone like the Jacinth of heaven, the color of sidereal fires. The pearls of Charity were upon him,—a chaplet of garnered tears! Love divine surrounded him with roses; and the whiteness of his Resignation obliterated all earthly trace.

Soon, to the eyes of the Seers, he was but a point of flame, growing brighter and brighter as its motion was lost in the melodious acclamations which welcomed his entrance into heaven.

The celestial accents made the two exiles weep.

Suddenly a silence as of death spread like a mourning veil

from the first to the highest sphere, throwing Wilfrid and Minna into a state of intolerable expectation.

At this moment the Seraph was lost to sight within the sanctuary, receiving there the gift of Life Eternal.

A movement of adoration made by the Host of heaven filled the two Seers with ecstasy mingled with terror. They felt that all were prostrate before the Throne, in all the spheres, in the Spheres Divine, in the Spiritual Spheres, and in the Worlds of Darkness.

The Angels bent the knee to celebrate the Seraph's glory; the Spirits bent the knee in token of their impatience; others bent the knee in the dark abysses, shuddering with awe.

A mighty cry of joy gushed forth, as the spring gushes forth to its millions of flowering herbs sparkling with diamond dew-drops in the sunlight; at that instant the Seraph reappeared, effulgent, crying, "Eternal! Eternal! Eternal!"

The universe heard the cry and understood it; it penetrated the spheres as God penetrates them; it took possession of the infinite; the Seven Divine Worlds heard the Voice and answered.

A mighty movement was perceptible, as though whole planets, purified, were rising in dazzling light to become Eternal.

Had the Seraph obtained, as a first mission, the work of calling to God the creations permeated by His Word?

But already the sublime hallelujah was sounding in the ear of the desolate ones as the distant undulations of an ended melody. Already the celestial lights were fading like the gold and crimson tints of a setting sun. Death and Impurity recovered their prey.

As the two mortals re-entered the prison of flesh, from which their spirit had momentarily been delivered by some priceless sleep, they felt like those who wake after a night of brilliant dreams, the memory of which still lingers in their soul, though their body retains no consciousness of them, and human language is unable to give utterance to them.

The deep darkness of the sphere that was now about them was that of the sun of the visible worlds.

"Let us descend to those lower regions," said Wilfrid.

"Let us do what he told us to do," answered Minna. "We have

seen the worlds on their march to God; we know the Path. Our diadem of stars is There."

Floating downward through the abysses, they re-entered the dust of the lesser worlds, and saw the Earth, like a subterranean cavern, suddenly illuminated to their eyes by the light which their souls brought with them, and which still environed them in a cloud of the paling harmonies of heaven. The sight was that which of old struck the inner eyes of Seers and Prophets. Ministers of all religions, Preachers of all pretended truths, Kings consecrated by Force and Terror, Warriors and Mighty men apportioning the Peoples among them, the Learned and the Rich standing above the suffering, noisy crowd, and noisily grinding them beneath their feet,—all were there, accompanied by their wives and servants; all were robed in stuffs of gold and silver and azure studded with pearls and gems torn from the bowels of Earth, stolen from the depths of Ocean, for which Humanity had toiled throughout the centuries, sweating and blaspheming. But these treasures, these splendors, constructed of blood, seemed worn-out rags to the eyes of the two Exiles. "What do you there, in motionless ranks?" cried Wilfrid. They answered not. "What do you there, motionless?" They answered not. Wilfrid waved his hands over them, crying in a loud voice, "What do you there, in motionless ranks?" All, with unanimous action, opened their garments and gave to sight their withered bodies, eaten with worms, putrefied, crumbling to dust, rotten with horrible diseases.

"You lead the nations to Death," Wilfrid said to them. "You have depraved the earth, perverted the Word, prostituted justice. After devouring the grass of the fields you have killed the lambs of the fold. Do you think yourself justified because of your sores? I will warn my brethren who have ears to hear the Voice, and they will come and drink of the spring of Living Waters which you have hidden."

"Let us save our strength for Prayer," said Minna. "Wilfrid, thy mission is not that of the Prophets or the Avenger or the Messenger; we are still on the confines of the lowest sphere; let us endeavor to rise through space on the wings of Prayer."

"Thou shalt be all my love!"

"Thou shalt be all my strength!"

"We have seen the Mysteries; we are, each to the other, the only being here below to whom Joy and Sadness are comprehensible; let us pray, therefore: we know the Path, let us walk in it."

"Give me thy hand," said the Young Girl, "if we walk together, the way will be to me less hard and long."

"With thee, with thee alone," replied the Man, "can I cross the awful solitude without complaint."

"Together we will go to Heaven," she said.

The clouds gathered and formed a darksome dais. Suddenly the pair found themselves kneeling beside a body which old David was guarding from curious eyes, resolved to bury it himself.

Beyond those walls the first summer of the nineteenth century shone forth in all its glory. The two lovers believed they heard a Voice in the sun-rays. They breathed a celestial essence from the new-born flowers. Holding each other by the hand, they said, "That illimitable ocean which shines below us is but an image of what we saw above."

"Where are you going?" asked Monsieur Becker.

"To God," they answered. "Come with us, father."

THE END